GWAHMP Canyon

INTO THE CAN

BY MARVIN GEEZEL

DORRANCE
PUBLISHING CO
EST. 1920
PITTSBURGH, PENNSYLVANIA 15238

Dorrance Publishing Co
585 Alpha Drive
Pittsburgh, PA 15238
Visit our website at *www.dorrancebookstore.com*

ISBN: 978-1-6393-7354-3
eISBN: 978-1-6393-7741-1

GWAHMP Canyon

INTO THE CAN

DEDICATED TO MY WONDERFUL *GRRLS*:
EDITH, RÉMY, IGGY
...AND MY BEAUTIFUL BRIDE, CARRIE.

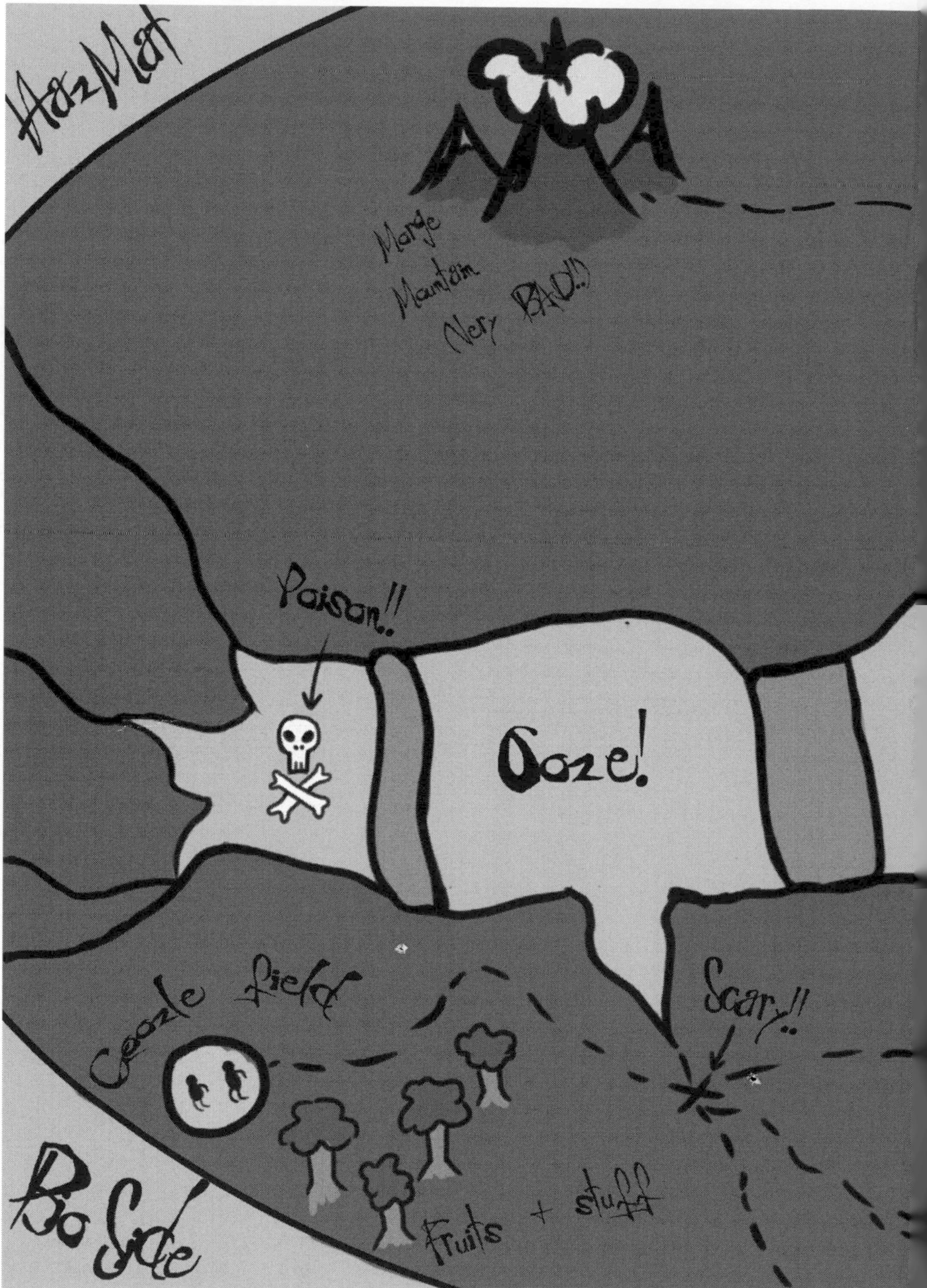
HazMat
Marge
Mountain
(Very BAD!!)
Poison!!
Ooze!
Goozle field
Scary!!
Fruits + stuff
Bio Side!

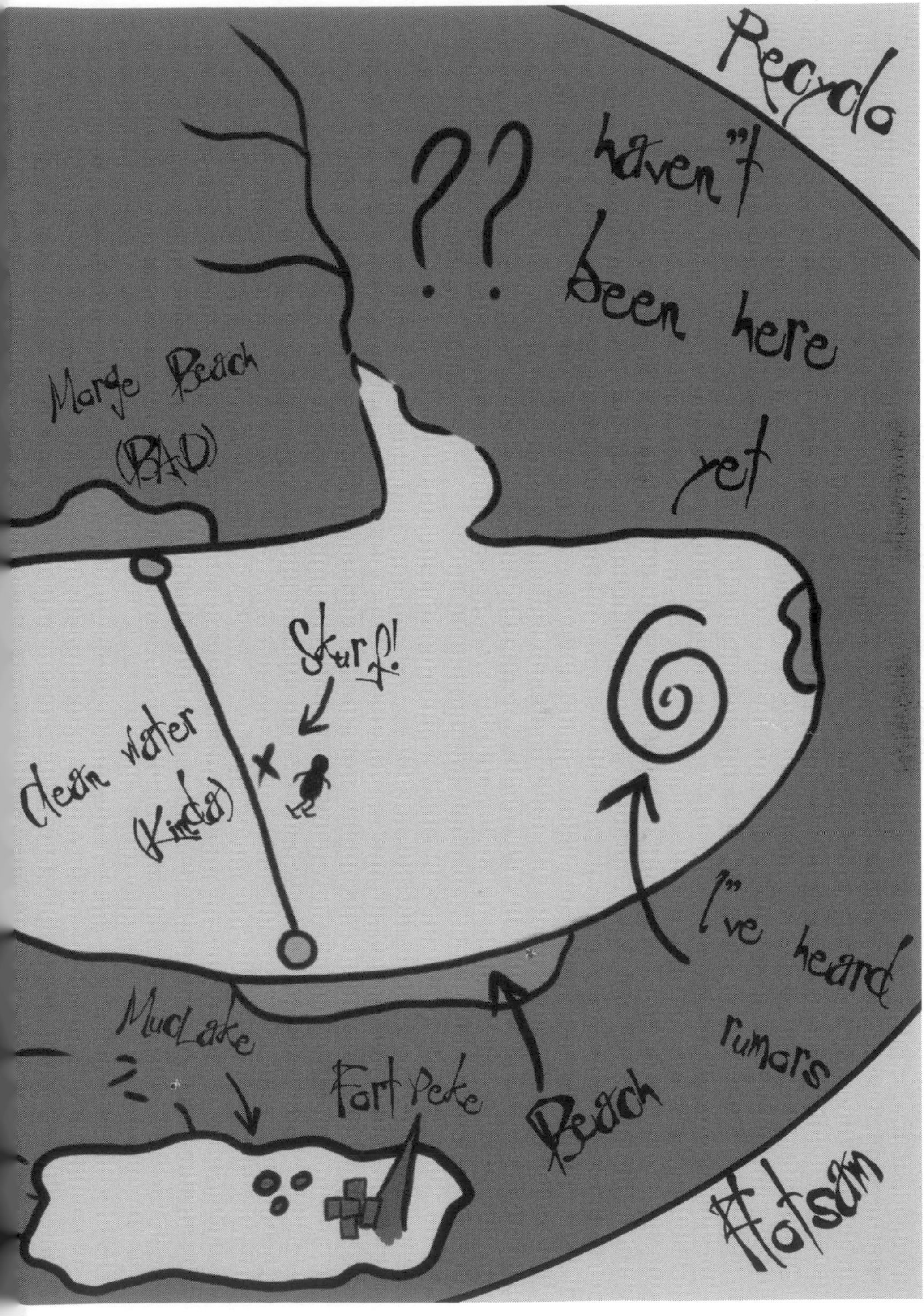
Recyclo
??
haven't been here yet
Marge Beach (BAD)
Skurf!
clean water (kinda)
I've heard rumors
MudLake
Fort Peke
Beach
Flotsam

Prologue

Belmont squatted shivering in the gloom of the steel dumpster. He listened with his eyes – rolling them wide from one side and then to the other. He couldn't hear – or see for that matter. But he sure could smell. The fumes from the seat of trash under his thighs were overpowering. He hugged his knees tighter to his chest and put his nose into his sleeve. The smell was horrendous, but this dumpster was the best hiding place he could quickly find.

After some time, as the tingling in his calves became hard to bear, he looked up towards a crack of pale light about four feet above him. It suggested daylight was approaching, but he couldn't be sure. At any rate, it was less dark out there than in the belly of this dumpster he'd been hiding in for an hour – or more.

Belmont slowly straightened to a hunch, and reached for the crack. He tilted his ear towards the gap for any sound. He heard nothing, but was startled by a large glop of wet trash falling from his backpack. His damp socks squelched in the muck as he shifted his shoeless feet.

He reached a tentative hand towards the lid, but quickly lost his nerve and told himself, "Just a few more minutes, just a few more…"

Then he heard a small scuffling outside of the dumpster. It was the scrape of metal on metal and a quiet clang of a chain. He was startled by the crank and whine of a winch motor and his scalp muscles crimped and his spine iced over.

"They found me. They know I'm here. Oh my garsh…I'm trapped."

He stood up and grabbed for the crack, but suddenly, the dumpster pitched backwards and he was thrown violently into the muck on the floor. He shouted through his wet hoodie that got entangled in his face, and then a block of trash fell towards him from the steel wall.

He was rolled backwards as the dumpster leaned perpendicular to the earth. Belmont wrestled with his clothes and the slanting, slick floor. When he righted himself he was pressing the bottom of the dumpster for support and the lid crashed open with a shattering gong.

"HELP!" he finally managed, but not as loud as the banging lid as trash rolled out of the mouth of the dumpster.

Belmont rolled out with the trash and landed hard. But a cushion of sludge helped break his landing – and fortunately not his ankle.

"HEELLLLP!!" he screamed again, but the noise was so consuming he wasn't sure he heard himself. He stood up and backed away from where he had landed. He was in a giant metallic container, similar to the dumpster, but five times bigger and open to the sky.

He looked at the top of the wall and watched his dumpster slowly dip below the horizon, while the sound of winches and banging metal lids echoed all around him.

A drizzle of debris from behind startled him. He ducked for cover just as another dumpster vomited its contents into the steel box. Another dumpster was starting to peek over the opposite side, and the lid crashed in and rang cataclysmic in his ears.

Six dumpsters in total poured around Belmont as he weaved back and forth to avoid being buried by the drifts of trash piling up around him.

"Can anybody hear me? I'm in here! Help! Help me!!"

The belch of a diesel engine and the sudden jolt of the massive waste hauling truck caused a few tons of garbage to shift and cascade into the center towards Belmont. He lost his footing, banged his head and crumpled into a heap as he was blanketed by a thin layer of refuse.

While Belmont was knocked unconscious, the waste hauler signaled left out of the alley and made an extremely broad turn into heavy traffic. He turned on the radio, shifted gears, engaged the automatic-driver and set in for a long relaxing drive to the seaport. Unaware of his unintended stowaway, the driver would dump his day's load onto the last trash barge out of port for the night, and he would be home for an unhealthy breakfast of dark coffee and bacon by 8 A.M.

Watching this unfold from a darkened doorway in the alley, a face, known to Belmont but unseen, smiled darkly. It watched as the waste hauler removed the cargo from the back streets of this posh neighborhood, towards its ultimate destination far in the Pacific Ocean. The face paused for a few moments pondering. Then, it quickly turned to go.

Sunny Day

One day, while on a much needed vacation, Dr. Herbert Warren Mumford, director of the Council of Earthly Affairs, was watching his son play on the beach. His son, Belmont, was a very inquisitive toddler – even more so than the average toddler. Belmont would often sit transfixed by a dangling chain or flag dancing in the wind, or a snail exchanging its shell for an empty tube of lip-balm. He would sit quietly studying the object with a determined single-mindedness. His focus was so intense that during these bouts, it was difficult to get him to respond to anything else.

His parents once left Belmont on the front lawn, staring at a fading pen-light. Some of his earlier breakfast was drying on his bib and attracted a group of Bigants (so called because they are, simply, Big-ants). The Bigants had decided that Belmont had more breakfast on him than could be picked off outside, so they hoisted him onto their collective backs, and started to march him away to their cave. Although his parents were attentive enough to notice immediately (and concerned enough to hire a Bigant exterminator the very next day) Belmont was so spellbound that he did not seem to notice at all.

Dr. Mumford and his wife had been concerned, but a handful of doctor appointments, tests and examinations later, he was diagnosed as being an extremely inquisitive and focused young boy (which is how the reader has already been introduced to Belmont) – but also extremely healthy.

That had been two years ago. A lot had changed for the Mumford family in that period of time, and much of it was not good.

Dr. Mumford bounced Belmont on his shoulder as they walked down the sand toward the shore, "Your mom used to love this beach. We came with you when you were just a baby – now look at you. Four years old and so big and smart."

"Of course there was a time when it wasn't so polluted…ahh, but let's not fret about that now."

Belmont sat engrossed by a bobbing tin can carried on the small waves of the shoreline. The tide would wash the tin can closer to his toes and then slowly pull the can back out again. Dancing in and then back out; each time the can would come close to his wriggling toes, Belmont's eyes would widen and a slight crease would develop in his baby brow.

The tin can eventually found its way to within Belmont's grasp, and his father had to move him back from the waves that carried an armada of cans, Styrofoam and disposable face masks.

Finding an uncluttered area proved to be a challenge as the litter was uncommonly heavy, even for this day and age.

"Well, Monty," Dr. Mumford said, "It appears as though we'll have to clear an area for ourselves.

Dr. Mumford set to clearing a space of a few feet, and surrounded the area with sand while Monty tried to help by reinforcing the walls with bits of rubbish and old popsicle sticks. When completed, they had a shallow depression about three feet across and a couple feet deep. Dr. Mumford watched Belmont crawl around in the space exploring a shovel handle here and an old Christmas ornament there. He sat back and stared at his son.

"Monty, I really am sorry that you have to grow up in an environment like this. I really don't know how we let the entire planet get into such a bad way. Mankind has ruined this planet, and…." He drifted off and had to take a moment to fight back tears. Monty paused in his play and looked at his daddy.

"…and it took her away from us. You lost your mommy because we let it get so bad. Because *I* let it get so bad. We provided a terrible environment for humans, and a perfect environment for disease and decay. and…and it took her away." The doctor paused again and collected his emotions. He breathed deeply and continued in a deliberate tone.

"But that is why I do what I can. That is why I am committed to working towards solving this pollution issue. Until we bring our waste issue under control, and fix some of the harm we have done to this beautiful planet – like some terrible house guests – I will not rest. I will not rest until we have solved this problem we caused."

"Daddy nappy time." Belmont said pointing at his father.

The doctor smiled sadly at his son and tousled his hair. "Yes, yes. I know, I get like this when I'm tired. I could probably use a little doze. Do you mind if Daddy lays down?"

Monty raked up a small sand pile next to him and patted it like a pillow.

"Ha. I think it may be a bit small in here. Daddy is going to lay right there," pointing outside the hole. "Monty should probably take a little nappy too, what do you think about that?"

Monty showed his father what he thought of that, by promptly ignoring him and went back to digging in the sand.

Doctor Mumford chuckled, handed him his favorite pail, and proceeded to take a catnap in the sun on the hood of a nearby old Buick that served as a beach-chair for him and his son.

Hole in the Ocean

His long days at the office and the warm sun made him lose track of time. He dozed comfortably but woke up with a start an hour later. The tide had risen to the edge of the small enclosure they had dug earlier to contain his son. Now, the drifting clutter was stacked up against the shallow walls. From his position, Dr. Mumford could not see his son.

"Monty. Monty! Hold on son, papa's coming."

He waded into the water, swooshing aside the floating debris, and peered into the hole. Panic set in immediately when he saw that, instead of his son, a few rotting boards and empty water bottles covered the bottom and leaned heavily on the side of the well.

"MONTY! Where are you, Belmont?"

Dr. Mumford hopped into the pit and frantically began flinging boxes and cola bottles aside as he looked for his son.

"Oh my garsh. Oh MY GARSH. Monty, please – where are you son? Where Are You…"

The Doctor's growing panic was immediately interrupted when his eyes met the soft eyes of his son, watching his father's strange movements from the hood of the Buick.

"Oh Belmont…the Heavens you're alright."

For the rest of the waning afternoon, the Doctor over comforted his already comfortable son – rocking him and petting his hair while they watched the tide continue to climb up the beach.

"Son, you scared me. I can't lose you, too. We'll clean this up. Not just the beach, but the whole world. And you'll help me. Wontcha son. You're gonna help me clean up this mess we made."

"We dug hole. Hole in the ocean." Belmont was watching the pit and grabbing at the air with a pudgy fist.

Dr. Mumford watched the water rise to the mouth of their little sand pit. There was a vast expanse of surface water covered with litter and then this strange hole right in the middle of the high tide. It did seem as though there was a hole in the tide.

As floating debris collected on the edge, it would fall into the bottom of the hole.

A small twitch started to dance on the end of Dr. Mumford's nose, and then a smile played across his lips.

"Hot Sauce!! That's it! I've got it... *we've* got it. Monty, that's the solution. A <u>hole</u> in the occan. Yes, that's it!"

He jumped up on the hood and started to dance. Belmont, never missing an opportunity to dance, stood up dancing and singing his favorite song. "*Ol' MacDonald had a farm...*"

"Hooya! Monty, we will dig a hole in the ocean!"

"We did Daddy. See daddy," pointing.

"No, Monty. Well, yes. Well. Yes, a *well*. We will dig a *well* in the ocean! The biggest, widest, deepest well that you can imagine. And that, Sarah Sylvia Cynthia Stout, is where we will take the garbage out!"

Dr. Mumford started to sing along with his son: "*Little Monty Dug a well, ei, i ei i 0, and in that well they put the trash, ei-i-ei-i-0...*"

Waking

Belmont was dreaming. All was safe and warm, like lying under heavy blankets of honey. There was a drowsy lullaby tinkling away in the distance as Monty floated pleasantly unconscious. *Ei-i-ei-i-o*

A slight tickling pressure developed on his forehead and he started to drift into wakefulness. As he passed from dream to reality, the pressure became sharper and sharper and soon evolved into a throb. He squinted a bit and tried to fight back into the sleep from which he was being dragged.

Soon his throbbing forehead was matched with a tingling in his left hand...and then tightness in both legs. What previously felt like blankets of honey now gained uncomfortable weight and his hand stung. Soon he felt compressed and he couldn't get a full breath. His numb hand burned as if being slowly cooked and his formerly tight legs felt like lead. Almost instantly, Monty's entire body ached and he was kicked awake by the pain.

Panting, his eyes flew open to see nothing but blackness. He struggled to get his bearings and found that he was pinned on his stomach with his left arm somehow behind him. He was completely disoriented by the darkness, a screaming headache and his awkward position. He tried to yell and found that his mouth was too dry to be of much help, and his chest too compressed to provide ample air. Panic grabbed him for a moment, and he thrashed his unmoving arms and legs. He jerked his head upwards, which amplified his already aching head when he bumped it – hard. *Thunk!*

Oddly, the sharp pain in his head calmed him a bit. He was forced to lay his head back to rest and take stock of the situation. As he already noted, he was pinned on his stomach with a sizable weight on top of him.

He soon realized he was not at all under a blanket of warm honey, but instead pinned under a mound of heavy garbage.

His nose was pushed up against a bar of metal which blocked all sight. His right arm was tucked under him, and his left arm was awkwardly twisted and pinned behind his back. While his right hand tingled, his left one burned with the lack of blood. He could practically hear his cells screaming for nourishment.

His legs seemed in normal location, just spread like a beached starfish. While he could wiggle them a bit, his pelvis was slammed tight to the floor, and didn't allow him much leverage. He also couldn't seem to bring them together as there was a large and sharp object between his knees. His legs were uscless to him. One ankle seemed to be able to rotate completely, so there was that.

Despite the ache he felt everywhere else, his face and cheek felt strangely cuddled. It was resting on something warm and fuzzy.

He tried to turn his chin, but whatever was immediately above his head was too close to the ground and didn't allow enough clearance. It was then he heard the pleasant tinkling again. Softly and soothingly, something was playing him a lullaby.

Ol' Macdonald had a farm…

He pushed at the softness with his cheek to try to move it with no success. He opened his mouth and pushed at the plushness with his tongue. He immediately regretted this move as he tasted the terrible tang of salty poop.

With a moo moo here and a moo…

He nodded his head forcefully and attempted to slide the fuzzy object out from under his head. Two nods, three nods and *poompff*: a dirty yellow plush rabbit came to stare eyeball to eyeball with Monty, while his face came to rest on a significantly less fuzzy handful of bottle caps.

Despite the discomfort, the half-inch of room allowed him to slowly roll his head around and face another direction. The movement cracked a few vertebrae in his neck and almost felt good. The new position relieved some pressure on his chest and he worked his right arm up towards his chin.

Panting, he laid his head on his hand and rested a bit. A lot of work fighting a plush toy and moving your hand. He rolled his head back around to be glared at by the bunny that immediately taunted him with a jingle.

Oink, oink here…

What seemed like hours later, Monty was able to get both arms "free" and into a push-up like position. He had to suffer while the blood came screaming back to his left hand and his nerves punished him for making them so thirsty for so long. But at last they were free.

He tried to push himself up, but the pressure on his back was far too heavy. He knocked it with his elbows a bit, and noted that it sounded like hollow wood. He gave it a couple of sharp raps, but didn't have enough room to give it a good whack.

Suddenly, he heard a faint sound in the distance. He strained to hear and thought it might be a voice.

Old MacDonald had a farm, ei ei o

"C'mon rabbit, shut up!"…the fuzzy rabbit seemed to enjoy irritating Belmont.

The Meeting

Were those voices in the distance? Yes, definitely voices...or at least *a* voice. Monty's heart skipped a bit and he started to gather his breath to yell for help.

"I know he came through here. I saw... *inaudible*..."

Was it a girl's voice?

"I don't know what it's doing in this part...*inaudible*...better not stay around... *inaudible*...catch him!"

They seem angry? Arguing?

"... *Inaudible*...is hunting? They don't really hunt here. No matter. If we find him, Magnus will string him up by his hairy big toe..."

Monty's breath caught in his already constricted chest. Maybe it would be better to be pinned under here than strung up by his toe.

Footsteps and shuffling noises became clearer and the voices sounded very close. She must be right above me, thought Monty.

"So what did you think of the finals? I personally think he got lucky... you're not going to say anything Magnus, what about you Apple?"

"Anything!" It was a second voice. Also female. Younger... actually very young. Like a kid or something.

At that moment, Belmont's plush nemesis decided to sing. *Quack, quack here and a quack quack there...*

"OMG dust-bunny, you little traitor," he thought.

The voices stopped and Monty held his breath. Seconds drifted by like waiting for a storm. Suddenly, a tiny hand shot down from beyond Monty's vision and grabbed the treacherous rodent's yellowed ear. Instantly, it disappeared into an empty patch above.

"Yay! You know I really like rodents. Especially Bunny BunBuns!" The little girl's voice again.

Someone laughed, "Thought you caught a Morge for a minute…let me see that toy…yeah, it's not as dirty as most. Okay, you can keep it. C'mon, we better keep going."

Belmont heard the rattling sound of something large being moved around above him and heavy footsteps.

Monty waited a few more seconds before he let his breath return to normal and he let himself relax a bit, before…

"WWHOOMP!!!" Suddenly, there was light everywhere as the massive weight on Monty's back was ripped upwards. The movement was so sudden that it caused an updraft of blowing dust, scraps of paper and bottle caps.

Monty scrambled to flip over, the sudden ability to move causing him no end of ache in simply rolling over. He shielded his eyes from the brightness and dust as he squinted up through the empty patch of garbage that he was lying in.

Above him stood a monster, a huge hulk of a man. His head gleamed golden, haloed by bright lights behind him so Monty could not see his face. But he saw the rest of him. His slightly bowed tree-stump legs were straddling Monty's bed of trash. His shoulders bulged above his outstretched bare chest the width of a kitchen table while two massive gorilla arms held a battered chest of drawers above his head. As the dust and light debris cascaded back down around Monty, the giant stood motionless holding this heavy piece of furniture threateningly above the prone Monty.

What a bit of luck to be freed from that weight only to be inevitably smashed by it from this…beast.

"Boo!"

A little sprite of a girl appeared standing on an iron girder that hung slightly over Belmont. She wore pink shorts under an orange skirt with a large bleach stain on the side, and a green T-shirt that said "Camp Counselor" on the chest. A few randomly placed pig-tails jutted out in her hair – and she was waggling a sharpened pipe at him.

"Her name is Eve, but we all call her Apple."

"Who…wha…what…" Monty cranes his neck around defensively, looking for the owner of the voice.

A slim girl about Monty's age was squatting next to the motionless giant on what seemed to be an overturned canoe.

She had frizzy brown hair tied up in a complex rat's nest on top of her head. It was tied with a bright green and red Christmas ribbon and the contrast seemed oddly nice to Belmont.

His first impression was "she's pretty". His second impression was "she's holding a spear at my nose".

"'Who, wha, what' indeed… 'who wha what' are you?" she says to him.

"Aaa… um… I ah," Monty stammered.

"Come on, out with it quickly – hard to make something up on the go, isn't it?" she twirled the spear at his eye level.

"No. Aaa, Belmonty. I mean Belmont, Monty."

She seemed to ponder this, but brought the spear point back a bit "well, which did you decide on then?"

Clearing his throat and saying more confidently, "My name is Belmont. People call me Monty."

"Well, we're people, so we'll call you Monty – until we know differently. As I said, that's Apple and I'm Rachel… People call me Rachel. So Monty, what brings you to the wonderful Can?"

Sparks

The two girls led the way. Belmont picked his way carefully, and slowly, through a tangled path of crates, boxes and jumbled wires while they nimbly walked and talked as though it were an open sidewalk.

They seemed to be trekking through a garbage dump or a heavily polluted field – which would not have been terribly uncommon to find. The path was well lit by these enormous stadium-style lights far above their heads. But they were so intense, that it was hard to see any distance for all of the shadows they cast, so Belmont couldn't really get his bearings.

The huge but silent man-boy followed behind Belmont. He was shouldering an overstuffed nylon pack. A sock and the handle of a pair of gripless pliers were peeking out of the top.

"Okay guys, we did pretty well foraging today. We got some not-so-terrible clothes, a pair of pliers, half a roll of duct tape – that was a huge win. We got some usable silverware and cups. A single size five shoe for Gilly, she'll be happy even if it doesn't match her other shoe.... What else?"

"BunnyBunBuns," the little girl said, and waved it in the air.

"Oh yeah, and a new pet. Two, if you count this one," the older girl said, hooking a thumb at Belmont and winking at Apple.

"Magnus and Apple you go ahead, I'll catch up with you after I locate our other two *friends*." The way she emphasized the last word made Belmont question her sincerity.

"I wanna come with you and Belmonty."

"But then Magnus won't tell the others about our new visitor…" she stopped when she saw Apple starting to pout. "Okay, fine. They'll be as surprised as we were."

With that, the colossus hoisted the bag, and lumbered down the path. The younger girl giggled, ducked into a stand of tires and disappeared from sight.

"Let's go meet our traveling companions, shall we."

———

A young boy was sitting slunch-backed in a broken rocking chair. He had his feet propped up on a stack of rusty pipes and was lazily bouncing a wet tennis ball against a rusty cross-beam. *Thwuck, catch, Thwuck, catch…*

Watching with penetrating eyes and every nerve wound to guitar-string tension was a wire-haired dog. The dog stood motionless with his pointed ears pricked and tongue hanging mid-pant. The dog had a barely noticeable movement of its eyes as they practically drilled holes into the bouncing ball. *Thwuck, catch, thwuck, catch…*

The dog was so wound to pounce that you could hear its nails titter against the broken slick of linoleum below its feet. Belmont thought for a moment he could see an aura of energy haloed around the animal.

The boy held onto the ball for a beat, breaking the rhythm of the *thwuck, catch, thwuck, catch…*

Very quickly, the boy flicked his wrist out, but held the ball firm. The dog's flank twitched, and the aura seemed to brighten.

Suddenly, the boy hurled the tennis ball into the yard, which caused an explosion of fur and dust. The dog ground its nails into the linoleum with four full lunges before its paws stuck and the dog took off.

The dog's legs flopped like untied shoes. You could see that its back legs were going a little faster than the front legs, and the beast got caught off balance. But the split second that its hairy rump hit the dirt, its front end resumed the lead position and dragged its downed-end into the race.

The dog had a bead on the slowly arching ball as it came down with a little puff of dust and a squelchy bounce. The dog needed only about four seconds to cover the thirty or so feet before its snout opened happily and clamped at the ball.

Its first snap closed on thin air with a big SNOP and a tiny sparkling of blue. Belmont rubbed his tired eyes, knowing he had to imagine it.

The mouth had barely shut before it opened again and snapped up the ball. The dog struggled to a stop and rolled over on itself before twisting impossibly and planting its paws on solid earth.

A single breath passed through the dog's dusty nose before it gathered up its energy and bounded back to the boy. It dropped its ball at the foot of the boy's chair and proceeded to turn into stone – its nose inches from the slobbery green fuzz of a ball. Again, the hazy blue halo humming from the dog's fur.

"That's Sparks…and Harrison."

Belmont looked sideways at Rachel. "Which is which??"

That teased a smile out of the girl. "Sparks is our friend there, and that's his mongrel Harrison."

She walked towards the couple and Belmont followed. As she approached his chair from behind, she said, "Hiya, Harry. Oh hey Sparks, I found you a new friend…"

The boy didn't look around and said, "Whatcha find, another rat? Or a drowned cat?"

"Yeah, something like that…a bit of both actually."

Belmont came into the boy's field of vision. He half-fell half-jumped out of his seat and lost the ball, which rolled away. The dog was immediately in the air darting for the ball and crashed into a set of crates while snapping up the ball with his teeth. Belmont knew this time that he saw a blue spark of energy escaped from the tips of the dog's ears.

"Who…wha…what…" he stammered wide-eyed from the chewed up length of linoleum.

"Oh man, not you too."

"What the… what the monkey is that?"

"Not 'what the monkey', *who* the monkey?"

"That's Belmonty," Apple suddenly arrived and poked her head out from the center of a stack of large worn tires. "He's Belmonty. He's from UpTop."

The boy stared for an awkward couple of seconds before jumping up and striding to where Belmont stood. With his gaze so intent, and his mouth half-open, he looked a bit like his dog. He walked up to Belmont staring at him like he was sizing him up, elevator eyes from foot to hairline and back down to stare directly into Belmont's eyes. Belmont eased back half an inch and sort of dropped his eyes a bit.

"I'm Belmont. It's, ah, nice to meet you, um, Sparks."

The boy glared deeper into Belmont's eyes and seemed to twitch his upper lip a bit and let out a sound that sounded like a slight growl.

"What's that?" he snarled.

"I, uh, said that I'm Belmont. Um, nice to meet you."

"*People* call him Monty. *You* should probably stick with Belmont," Rachel shouted to the boy.

"Hruumph." He snorted, and turned away towards Rachel. "So where'd you fish this one out of?"

Rachel shrugged her shoulders and vaguely gestured with a flap of her hand. "Over by the east quarter. He stinks worse than your dog, Harry."

"Hey, it's not my fault…" Belmont retorted.

"Yeah, well you found him, you can clean him." With that he righted his chair and wedged it back into place, sat back down and reached for the gooey tennis ball, which the dog seemed to drop as if on cue.

"And the *dog* is named Sparks…I'm Harrison…"

Belmont stammered and looked over to Rachel, who tried to conceal an impish grin.

With this awkward exchange, Belmont felt he needed to have a better introduction. He sat down on an upturned bucket and said, "Okay, let's have it out. I'll tell you how I got here, and then you tell me why you are here. Oh… and *where* is here?"

"Here? You mean you don't know? Look around you. Notice any common elements?"

"Well, it's dirty."

"Ya think?? Some might even say it's trashy. This is all garbage. This is the *ultimate* garbage dump. You, my little drowned rat, are in The Can."

Belmont's face fell and went pure white. He sputtered a bit and stared without seeing.

"Yep," Harrison swept his arm upwards to the lights "Welcome to the Global Waste and Hazardous Material Processing center. GWAHMP Canyon – home of the world's finest refuse."

At just that point, as if to punctuate Harrison's sarcastic welcome, the stadium lighting far above them turned off with a loud electric *BONG*. They were plunged into inky darkness for maybe five seconds before a curtain of light descended upon them. The sun had breached a horizon that stretched far above them with grand effect.

Instantly, the dizzyingly high sleek walls of the canyon were visible. They towered above the little group of kids, stretching to forever and somehow making the sun appear smaller because of it.

Belmont promptly fainted.

Something's Wrong

It was very early in the morning. Monty normally slept soundly, and waking before dawn was foreign to him. Those rare times he did, he usually rolled over, snuggled his pillow and conked out again quickly. This morning, he heard his dad talking loudly on the phone.

Coordinating and developing the massive waste treatment project had been Dr. Mumford's life work for almost a decade. Belmont was used to his dad's late hours with his firm, the Global Waste And Hazardous Material Processing Company, or GWAHMP Co. They had been constructing and managing its major project, GWAHMP Canyon, for the better part of eight years, ever since that inspiring afternoon on the beach.

But his dad always handled the work with passion and excitement. This morning, however, his dad's voice sounded distressed.

Monty crept downstairs in his socks. He found his dad holding the phone up to his ear as though it were going to bite him. His face was pale and his mouth hung open almost as wide as his eyes.

"Oh my" was the only phrase he uttered after a very long time.

He seemed to listen some more and said, "Yes, yes. We will talk about how to close the facility when you get here."

He dropped his arm, but didn't set the phone down for a long moment.

"Dad? Dad, are you okay?" Monty asked him, concerned.

"Oh, those poor people. Their poor families." The doctor whispered, barely audible to Monty's ears.

"Dad, what's wrong? What people? Whose family?"

The doctor seemed to focus for a moment on Belmont's face. "Oh Belmont, it's terrible. The Facility. GWAHMP Canyon. It's hurting people."

"Dad, what are you talking about?"

"Monty, The Facility. It's dangerous. Hazardous. Our workers are being injured...or *changed*!" he choked on the last word, before picking up the phone again and dialing.

"Lucy, it's Herb. When you get this, call me. No. Better yet, I'm coming to pick you up... I have terrible news."

Lucy was the doctor's most trusted colleague. She was always the one that he called whenever there was a problem that the doctor could not seem to fix immediately.

He grabbed his coat off the back of the chair, rushed to the front door, and put his hand on the knob. But he paused and turned to Monty.

"Belmont. Something terrible has happened that I don't understand. But we'll fix it. We always do. But remember, I love you and always will. Now go back to bed. I'll be back soon." Then he whipped open the door and was gone.

"Changed?!" Monty thought to himself. "Our workers? At the facility?" He immediately thought about his best friend Louis, downstairs. Louis's mom worked for the company for as long as Monty could remember. He knew she was currently stationed at The Can. He was worried about Louis and his family and decided to go warn him, despite the hour of night.

But warn him about what? What does 'changed' mean, really?

Monty climbed through his bedroom window into a chute he had made that allowed him to sneak out of his bedroom window. It dropped him quickly to an escape landing a few floors below him. He crawled out of the exit of the tunnel, rapped on the nearby window and waited.

Louis was always a good friend to Belmont. He was quiet and a bit of a bookworm, but that seemed to work well for their friendship. Belmont wasn't exactly outgoing, or the most popular kid on the playground. They were very comfortable in each other's company.

Without waiting too long, Louis slowly raised the window shade and Monty could tell he had been crying.

"Louis, what's wrong?"

"Oh. Nothing. I wasn't... I mean, I'm not. I mean, I'm fine," he said, rubbing his eyes and sniffing loudly.

This made Monty more nervous for his friend and he blurted out.

"Louis, my dad tells me there's something terrible going on at The Can. Have you talked to your mom?"

"No!" He responded excitedly. "She hasn't called. She hasn't called in four nights. My Nana is worried, 'cause she always calls at dinner-time. And now it's been four days. We are so worried about her." His voice cracked, and tears formed fresh in his red-eyes.

"You tried to call her?"

"Yes, but she didn't answer. But that's typical. Her phone only works when she's on topdeck. You know, it's too far underwater for her to have service..." he trailed off.

"Louis, I'm going upstairs to get changed for school. My dad is having Lucy and some of the people from the firm over. Once I know more, I'll come down and tell you. And then we can go to school together."

Louis composed himself and wiped a sleeve across his nose. "Yeah. Okay, that's a good idea. Thanks. Let me know as soon as you know something. I'll see you in a few hours."

Monty climbed back up the chute, looking down at the alley below him. Down there were a line of dumpsters and garbage cans waiting for the weekly pick up. It was hard for him to imagine that the same garbage would be collected, processed and sent down a massive well thousands of miles from here. Thousands of miles from anywhere, actually.

And that place was changing people into... *what*??

Monty changed in his room and packed his school backpack. Remembering that he had gym in about five hours, he added a pair of socks and shoes to the books, notepads and other school supplies already in the bag.

He looked around for anything else needed for school and his eyes landed on a hand-drawn map of GWAHMP Canyon's ground floor. Belmont had drawn it, but he had pretty much memorized the layout; The elliptical landmass was broken into four quadrants separated by water treatment lakes.

It was a good design. Actually a great design. It had been working so well towards fixing the planet's pollution problem. It was hard to believe that this place was causing such a commotion.

After a moment, he threw in a few packs of licorice rope, knowing they were Louis's favorite. He hoisted the backpack onto his shoulders, grabbed the ancient and used cell phone that his dad had given to him, reluctantly, when he turned twelve, and left his room.

He immediately heard arguing from his dad's study. While he had been gone, the doctor had apparently returned with guests.

Monty snuck to the corner of the stairs where he could barely peek into the study. He heard his dad, but couldn't see him. He did see Lucy sitting against the desk looking worried, and talking quietly to the man next to her.

Monty identified this man as Dr. Peele, and his stomach turned. Monty never liked Dr. Peele. He found him to be smarmy, slick and always hiding something behind that little switch of a mustache. A host of bad words came to Monty's mind the moment he saw the doctor.

He heard a new voice, and a man Monty did not recognize stood up from his dad's desk chair.

"It is far too expensive to just shut this down, Herbert. And it is far too expensive to fix at this point. The Facility can work on auto-pilot for a while. We can address your… concerns…later."

"My *concerns*?" His dad practically yelled. "Later?? I have some very good friends that work there. These are people! I am responsible for them. I am responsible to their families…"

"Well, I agree with you there. *You* are responsible for this, um, incident. And we want to help *you* avoid any trouble. That is why we are recommending our course of action."

There was a long pause in conversation before his dad responded in a very clear, yet very firm, voice.

"I *am* responsible for this, and I *will* take that responsibility. But I will not waste another moment with people in danger. Shut it down now, or I swear I will…"

"What? You swear you'll do what?" Sneered the new man.

Dr. Mumford stepped into view and got very close to the new man's face.

"I will call the press. Then we will be *forced* to address this issue publicly. And if you try to stop me…"

Lucy stepped up and put a calming hand on the doctor's shoulder. "Herb, come help me bring in the blueprints from my car. We can resume this conversation when we've all caught our breath a bit."

The doctor lingered for a moment longer, staring daggers at the new man. Then he relaxed a bit and left the room with Lucy.

Monty ducked his head behind the banister and waited for them to pass. He was going to follow his dad into the kitchen, and then the other men started talking to each other.

"He'll be ruined."

"Yes he will. But so will we. He doesn't seem to appreciate the amount of money we're talking about here."

"He's got us over a barrel. He doesn't seem to care about his career or money. He's too honest and stubborn."

"He does have us over a barrel, or over *a Can* as the case may be. Which is why we need to align our interests. We need something he does care about. Something we can hold over him. Leverage our position, if you will. Something to keep hidden, so he keeps our secret hidden. Something…or someone."

"The kid." Dr. Peele hissed loudly. "Of course"

The conversation shocked Belmont, and his phone fell out of his hands and hit the steps. With a loud thump-thump, the battery popped loose from his obsolete phone and fell to the floor before Belmont could grab his now worthless phone.

Both men looked up from the desk and immediately stared in Belmont's direction.

"And there he is!"

Belmont panicked. He grabbed his backpack and ran back up the stairs. He heard footsteps coming up behind him and he slammed his door. The handle immediately jiggled hard and Belmont made for the window and the attached slide that led to Louis's landing. As he was shoeless, he slid too quickly down the chute and landed hard on the fire escape.

He wasn't thinking clearly but had a vague notion that he would run to the front of the apartment and get his dad, who must be out front with Lucy. As he rolled out of the bottom of the chute to Louis's window, he realized he'd have to make it down the alley to the front of the block and around to the front of his house. It was longer than he wanted to run in his socks, but he didn't think about shoes while escaping and he didn't have time to get his gym shoes out of the pack.

Monty thought about knocking on Louis's window, but knew he wouldn't have much time to wait. He also didn't want to get Louis caught up in this mess. Instead he rolled towards the edge of the landing, swung his feet down and leapt the ten feet to the ground. He landed and rolled on the pavement below, skinning his knee. He got to his feet and looked up at the window.

Above him he saw the leering face of Dr. Peele. He was on the phone talking loudly. They made eye contact.

"Get out of the car and get the boy. He's in the alley. I'm coming down now," he growled into the phone. And then his face disappeared back into the bedroom.

Monty looked down the alley and saw a black SUV parked there. The driver's door opened and a large man got out and looked in the opposite direction of the alley.

Belmont needed a place to hide and fast, but there was really only one place to do it. He gathered a deep breath, and dove into a nearby dumpster.

Fort

"**B**elmonty... wakey wakey." Apple was standing over him dangling a piece of string tickling his nose.

He groaned, muscles feeling tight and his head hurting as much as it had from the night before. All of a sudden he recalled his predicament and sat upright.

"GWAHMP Canyon! We are in danger. This is a terrible place to be. We have to evacuate. In fact, it's supposed to have been evacuated."

Harrison was flipping a splinted baseball bat and looked over, "No duh about the danger thing – thanks for your insight. This one is especially sharp," he hooked a thumb in Belmont's direction.

"Oh, and I've lost my backpack. Where is my backpack? I need it for school... and Louis, I have to talk to Louis." Belmont was working himself up into a panicked state.

Rachel came over and spoke soothingly, "Belmont, seriously, we know. We know this is a dangerous place and we want to leave. But we haven't seen another person in...well, quite some time...and, well evacuate? We would like to leave as soon as we can but, um, there is no way out of here."

"And there is no one else to evacuate," she continued. "No workers have come down here that we've seen."

Harrison jumped in, "I mean, what kind of person builds this monstrosity and doesn't have security to make sure people don't get stuck in it. I wouldn't

27

mind meeting them 'cause I have a few words for them!" For punctuation, Harry slammed his bat into a rotted barrel.

Belmont gulped when he saw Harrison's violent response to The Can. He decided not to bring up his or his father's involvement at this particular time.

"Can I tell you something…we are safe. We're safetysafe. The fort is all safey." Apple cheerily skipped around them.

"She's right. Let's get back to the fort. We didn't find much today," Harrison looked at Belmont before finishing, "nothing important, anyway."

"Wanna go home, boy?" He said to the dog.

With the mention, the dog's ears prick up. This time Belmont quite clearly saw a spark of blue electricity arc between the tips of the ears. Now the name resonated with him.

Seeing Belmont's reaction, Rachel said, "Meet the world's most staticy dog."

"Ahh…Sparks. I get it now. Nice trick. Thanks for making that awkward." He mumbled.

———

They walked a short way talking before they reached an especially crowded section of trash. They lined up to walk in a single file line.

"Sorry we didn't see your backpack. Maybe we can go foraging near where we found you some other time. For now, we'd like to get back before the others worry," Rachel had been much kinder since Belmont's panic attack upon finding out he was in the bottom of a miles deep landfill.

As they rounded a corner of piled high bricks, Harrison said, "This is the beginning of Fort. This place offers some protection from the elements and, ah, stuff." He opened an old rusty car door attached to a swiveling post. It seemed to serve as a gate.

"It's safey, it's fun and safetysafe." Apple ran forward as the happily skipping leader.

The ground was moist here. Gunky mud started to grab at their feet and made rude noises when it let go.

Apple was bounding ahead through a twisting trail of half-submerged car parts, crates and discarded furniture that wound through the thick mud. At one point, she hopped up onto a desk chair to grab a hanging ladder. She monkey-barred over a ten foot gap in the tail, and gracefully hopped down on the other side.

The rest followed with Belmont in the rear.

"Are you out of breath?" asked Rachel, her hand on the first rung of the vertical ladder.

"No," Monty said, breathlessly.

Monty continued to follow, struggling a bit to keep up, but mostly because his arms and legs were still aching from his night under the dresser.

They rounded a few bends in the trail through the trash and came to an opening.

"So there's our fort. Headquarters of the JYKs."

"JYKs?" Monty asked.

"Ya, JYKs," Harrison said, and he moved forward around Apple, who was bouncing her new bunny friend on a large steel spring nearby.

"JYKs. J - Y - Ks. Junk Yard Kids. He likes to call us all that, but no one else really does. I think it sounds like *chicks*, and I <u>hate</u> that word." Rachel growled.

In front of them, a small island of garbage rose from a marshy moat of muck. Upon approaching the island, Monty noticed that the little band of kids didn't approach it directly, instead they started to circle around it. The mud started to get deeper and more aggressively pulled at their shoes. Soon, the trail turned into a path of trash through the oozing mud. They would hop from a sunken refrigerator to a broken pallet to a pile of broken cement and other rubble.

"Don't fall off. It gets really bad down there." Rachel said over her shoulder.

"Yay. Too sticky icky for kiddies," Apple chucked a rock into the muck and it sank slowly with a bloop. "And for bunnies," she waggled her fuzzy bunny towards the mud.

Belmont thought he saw something slither under the surface of the brown ooze where the rock landed. But maybe his lack of sleep was playing tricks on his eyes.

There was a slight rise in the land ahead of them. Perched on this tiny hill was the small mountain of trash that he had seen from the trailhead. They made their way towards it now, and hopped off their final stepping stone onto drier land.

The fort from the outside looked like an immense mountain of garbage. Maybe a bit more oddly shaped. Maybe a bit "chunkier", but still similar to the other piles of trash around them.

"That's the point, innit?" said Harrison, sensing Monty's thoughts. "It's supposed to blend in. Kinda camouflaged. Keep it hidden."

"Stop chatting and follow close." Rachel snapped, "This is where it gets really tricky."

Belmont, feeling extremely tired now, but not wanting to show it replied, "Listen, if a toddler can do it, I'm sure I'll manage."

Apple heard the comment and made a pouty face. She immediately scurried up a short rope ladder, swung across to a long piece of timber above and deftly balanced across it, skipped over a slippery slant of old siding and stopped about twelve feet up in a broken window pane.

"*Pbbbtttt!*" she shook the plush toy in his direction while sticking out her tongue.

"Ha, well you said it. After you." Rachel motioned to Belmont to follow after.

"Um, okay then."

After a much much much harder time, Belmont finally made it to the siding. He jumped over, but landed a bit on the slope, and lost his balance. He immediately started to slide down and noticed for the first time how far the slope fell.

He was caught on his arm by Harrison. While being pulled back up to safety, Belmont looked down as a loose shoe slid far down the side of the hill right into a patch of ooze. A second later, a small slimy creature surfaced and glommed onto the shoe, dragging it under with it.

"What the heck was that?" he asked as he climbed through the open window.

"The slide… or the MugSlug?"

"Um, I guess you answered my question. MugSlug? Are they dangerous?"

"You keep asking that question – keep using that word. I think we need you to understand something here. Everything is dangerous. All the animals, all the garbage, all the paths and all the Morges. *Everything* is dangerous. So buck up and act like a JYK!"

Once inside, the sheer magnitude of the structure became evident. The entire side of the mountain was a maze of crawlspaces and tunnels; a web of ropes and chain links. It was a virtual habitrail buried into a pile of trash.

He kept following the little pack into the side of the mountain. Often they were going upwards, but equally as often it felt as though they were sliding downward.

Upon entering the window pane, it was very dark. And then it got even darker as they made their way upwards. But then Monty started to notice reflections and a faint glowing light at certain turns in the path. Once he reached out to one of the lights and saw that it was a shiny bit of metal. Again he reached out further up and saw it was a shard of broken mirror.

While he was looking at the reflection, the party in front of him stopped abruptly. Just as abruptly, Monty bumped his nose right into the bum of Rachel.

"Watchit there!" She barked.

"Oh, I uh, oh," Monty stammered.

She turned back to the front of the tunnel. "Well, we're here."

Rachel shuffled to her feet in a crouched position and then jumped. Belmont scurried to where she disappeared and saw her sliding down an old corkscrew playground slide. She reached the bottom in full stride and immediately started chatting loudly.

"Is Magnus keeping the balls within the field? Don't let Martin cheat again! Who's winning?"

Belmont reached the edge of the path, and looked out. He was stunned by the size of the room. No, not a room, more like a complex or a small campus.

What appeared as a relatively medium sized structure on the outside, seemingly opened up into a clearing roughly the size of a basketball court (the comparison was made easier by an unpainted backboard and netless hoop hanging on one side of the field).

Loosely scattered throughout the floor were various clumps of riff-raff… both materials and individuals.

There was a small group of kids milling about little handmade flags, and Rachel was walking towards them.

The giant of a person that Belmont saw earlier was lining up to hit a blue rubber ball when a much smaller boy of about nine or ten hit a pink ball into the blue ball causing it to fall into a little funnel.

The giant frowned at the other boy, when someone said, "No. He's cheating. He's cheating again. It wasn't your turn." It was a young girl with dirty reddish pigtails sticking practically straight out from her head. "Rachel, he's cheating again."

"No-uh. I have the lead ball. I get an extra turn and I'm using it…" But while the girl was accusing the boy, the ball was heard to be rolling through the funnel, dropped into a bit of plastic piping, spun out wildly and hit a frying pan with a loud gong. Then it slowly rolled into a small hole in the ground.

"HA! We won! Me and Magnus won!!" A redheaded, pigtailed girl jumped slightly in the air and did a tiny fist-pump. "Yay us!"

The giant didn't move much except to lumber over and pluck the tiny little ball up with his gigantic fingers and drop it into the first boy's hand – and then leave his hand open wide. His palm was almost the size of the dangling frying pan.

"Fine, here. And the first boy dropped the pink ball into his hand."

"Okay. So team Gilly and Magnus now have the lead ball. We play them next, so who's got the next game…" she trailed off as she noticed them all staring past her at the newcomer.

"Wha…"

"Dat's Belmonty," Apple chirped, bouncing up from under a box somewhere.

"Yes. Belmont, meet the Junk Yard Kids."

"JYKs!!" shouted Harrison from behind them.

Dinner

There were many questions, but Belmont didn't have much to give them. He had been hit on the head while hiding in a dumpster, and then he woke up under a bookcase.

They seemed to be settling into an evening routine. A few of the kids were preparing what smelled like a meal. One kid, about seven or eight, who chattered in Spanish, puttered about and brought out a plate of food. A second boy of the same age, and pretty much the same exact look, started poking at a fire that was smoldering within a chunk of large cement sewage pipe.

They all slowly convened around the fire pit. The hole was hissing a thick white steam and randomly, orange sparks would belch from the pit. As Belmont leaned in closer, he could see that the fire was actually a small rolling mass of molten rock.

"That's Magma. She's our Cooky."

"Yes. Our oven, stove, campfire. It never goes out... but it sometimes burps." one of the two twins said as another small pop of sparks issued up.

Rachel, Apple and Harrison sat down around the fire and the redheaded girl, Gilly was futzing with some string on a damaged guitar.

He was served a plate of food (that surprisingly tasted pretty good). It looked like beans, grilled apples and corn bread.

There were seven kids here. Ranging from Apple at about four or five to the leviathan Magnus who could've been twenty-five for all he knew (he was actually only fourteen). Then there was Dante and Martin. Twins. Although one couldn't speak English and one could (that was a little odd). There was Harrison whom he had met before (and didn't seem to warm up to him any better than he had then) and quiet Gilly, who seemed to have a faint accent. Maybe Australian.

Then there was Rachel. Sassy, snappy and quite pretty Rachel. Belmont tried to sit next to her, since he knew her the best, he thought, but ended up sitting awkwardly on Magnus's huge knee. He flinched forward and sat hard on a bucket squeezed between him and Sparks. The dog stared intently at a wet tennis ball immediately in front of him, occasionally snatching a morsel of food out of the air that was tossed by one of the other kids while blue energy twinkled from its ears.

Gilly started playing the broken guitar (that surprisingly sounded pretty good). It was a nice background noise to the pleasant dinner. Monty couldn't believe how hungry he was and he wolfed down two plates of food before others looked at him.

"How long were you under that bookcase?" Asked one of the twins (possibly Martin, Belmont thought).

"I don't know. It felt like forever, but maybe it was a few hours. I really don't remember...."

This sparked the memory of hiding in the dumpster earlier that morning – or was it yesterday. Then his heart missed a beat when he realized he had lost his backpack. He patted his pockets and felt he still had his phone, but he knew it was uncharged and without a battery – utterly useless.

"Well, it would take well over a day to sail here. No wonder why you're so hungry. Do you want something more substantial to eat? We don't have much to choose from, but Dante here is a great cook...even if he can't putter-put."

The one called Dante flicked a bean at his brother and stuck out his tongue.

"No, just some more of those apples please, they're delicious." Belmont looked around him and a thought occurred. "Wait, where does the food come from? We're in a garbage dump; people don't throw away perfectly ripe apples. Are we eating garbage??" Monty spit the apple back onto the chipped ashtray he was using as a plate.

"*Si vuelves a decir que mi comida es basura, será la última vez que la pruebes, amigo mío.*" Dante responded angrily to Belmont.

"Easy Bro," his brother said to him, and then to Monty, "You'd be surprised what perfectly good things people throw away. Frankly, we've made a livelihood depending on it." He raised a large chipped dinner plate he was using. "But no, the apples don't come from the garbage…well not exactly anyway."

"Where then?"

Martin began to answer but Harrison cut him off. "…he's eaten enough of our food already, why don't we make him find out for himself?"

The others looked around, and then nodded.

"Actually, not a bad idea. A group of us were going foraging tomorrow anyway. We could use the extra hands." Gilly said.

"Too soon. I don't want to have to save him from himself – I mean, we found him under a bookshelf a few hours ago. Maybe in a few days." Rachel replied. "Apple, were you going to come with us, or stay here with Sparks?"

A slight snore was the only answer. Apple had fallen asleep in an old car seat lined with a gray sweatshirt.

A huge shadow started to slowly arc across the clearing. Far above, the sun was starting to set behind the west rim of The Can's surface floor.

With the long day (or days) Monty had, coupled with a full belly, warm fire, soft guitar and dwindling conversation, Monty felt his own eyelids drooping.

Yawn, "So how did you find this place?"

Harrison looked up angrily, "Find?? You think a perfect work of architectural genius like this just happens to arrange itself?? We made it. We found this little sorta island of dry land in MucLake. Then we heaped trash for walls to sleep out of the rain. And then we carved out more sleeping quarters. Cleared out lounging spaces and eating spaces and putter-putt spaces and, um, bathroom spaces. We tunneled out hallways and catwalks between these spaces. We erected walls and bridges and slippery slopes and false doors and teetering footpaths and trip riggings and trickiness at every conceivable access point. We built every hallway, every obstacle, every booby trap. We basically evolved a random smattering of junk into a multi-leveled, multi-faceted, multi-awesome labyrinth of garbage.

"We made it safe from unexpected visitors.... A fat lot of good it did us with you." Harrison ended his sentence by looking angrily at Belmont.

Belmont had dozed off and hadn't noticed Harrison's glare. But he jerked awake mumbling, "Sleeping quarters?"

"Ha. More insults falling on more deaf ears. Looks like there's one more person to ignore you, Harry." Rachel reached over and nudged Apple who was starting to suck her thumb. "C'mon lazy bones, let's show our new guest where we sleep."

SnoreTown

Belmont was too tired to do anything but follow Apple and Rachel through a few twists in a path before entering a huge cavernous space. The room was enclosed on all sides by towering piles of crushed cars.

Far above them, a patchwork of tarps were strung across providing them with a makeshift ceiling. It served to lessen the light from the electrical stadium lights that had kicked on soon after ShadowSet, their term for when the sun set behind the rim of the canyon.

"Don't worry, the lights go off in a few hours. It will be plenty dark in here for you." Rachel had noticed Belmont staring upwards.

But that was not what had grabbed his attention. It was the stacks of mattresses built in the center of the room. Each tower had more than a dozen stained, fraying and torn mattresses stacked one on top of the other. The shortest one was at least ten feet tall. A few looked to be more than fifteen.

Apple grabbed a knotted rope, kicked off her mismatched shoes and began scaling the automobile wall. She stopped on a jagged ledge and then leaped out holding the rope. She swung wildly above the mattress towers and then let go. Belmont gasped as she plummeted down squealing, and then saw her land in a splash of pink blankets and fuzzy animals.

"Welcome to SnoreTown," Rachel pointed at an old sign that read:

"Snore Town – Firm Mattresses 50% off Now Thru Sunday" that leaned against a stack of piled mattresses.

She grabbed the rope and duplicated what Apple just did, but with more grace and less squealing.

"C'mon up. There are two empty beds. Be careful not to land on us."

Belmont gulped and then shakily grabbed the rope. He was a few cars below Apple's ledge when he looked over to the towers.

"Yo. Go higher. That won't do it." Rachel shouted.

He climbed to Apple's perch and then looked back over. He was terrified, but also so darn tired.

"Here goes," he thought, and then leapt.

"Okay, looking good. Now let go!"

Monty did nothing of the sort. He slipped down a few knots in the rope with his feet waving aimlessly below him.

"No, you missed. Watch out…" but it was too late. He quickly passed the mattress towers and was arching back around.

"Oh no! You're too low!"

Belmont swung wildly back towards one of the taller towers. He smacked into the side of it and let go. He fell down a few feet and landed softly on a bed a few mattresses lower.

"Well, that was the right bed… but maybe not the right approach." Slowly the taller tower was tilting from Belmont's impact. It leaned dangerously, but then came back slowly, slowly slowly leaning the other way. It teetered a bit more, and then came to a rest.

"Well that was close. Harry would not have been happy with that."

Belmont started to answer, and fell asleep mid-sentence.

Sometime late in the night, Belmont woke to a very loud yell and watched as the tallest tower teetered, toppled and tossed its inhabitant across the floor. Harrison stood up bewildered and red-faced. "What the *helicopter* happened… "

"Would you be quiet – you sound like the princes with the pea." Rachel snapped.

Belmont wearily offered a quiet apology that wasn't heard by anyone, and fell back into a deep sleep.

First Day

"**W**akey-wakey," Apple was bouncing on the mattress next to Belmont's jiggling, and aching, body. Her jumping was causing the entire mattress tower to wobble.

"Alright, alright. I'm awake. I'm awake."

Belmont looked down and saw Harrison, Dante (or Martin?) and Magnus restacking mattresses from the pile that toppled the night before. Harrison and the twin would grab each end and hoist it up together. Magnus was a bit more efficient by heaving two at a time onto the growing stack.

"Harry was a little careless last night when he came to bed. Seems he landed a little, um, wrong, and knocked his tower over." Rachel winked at Belmont.

"It's never happened to me before," he growled, and looked suspiciously at Belmont.

"Yes, yes. Um, can I tell you something? Remember when, um, you did it before and knocked over, um, you knocked over Magnus's bed *and* my bed?" Apple offered helpfully.

"Well...it wasn't my bed. Never happened to *my* bed," he tossed his last mattress and Magnus had to finish the rest of the pile as the top was out of reach for the others.

"I told you not to stack it too high. So there you go. Maybe you'll learn to listen." Rachel scaled down her bed-tower to the bottom and walked through a broken door frame that served as the entrance to this bed room.

Rubbing sleep from their eyes and yawning, the JYKs were slowly gathering around the fire pit – Magma – for breakfast.

Martin was coming out of an opening in the surrounding walls of trash with a plate brimming with…fried eggs?!?

"Oh, Yes!" Harry said excitedly. His mood changing with the smell of breakfast. "What's the occasion, Dante?" He rubbed his hands together and sat down.

He responded in Spanish and gestured to Belmont.

"Oh. To *celebrate* our new *guest?*" he spat, but devoured his eggs hungrily.

"Scrambled Goozel eggs – yum dilly-um," Gilly said. "You'll want to wrap your laughing gear 'round these," she said to Belmont.

"GoodyGood!" Apple clapped and jumped into the empty car seat where she had fallen asleep the night before.

Belmont was trying to be polite, but had a very important question to ask. "I, uh, wonder if, um…you could tell me."

Some eyes turned towards him over their helpings of eggs.

"Where could I, um…"

"Out with it, Mumbles," Rachel said.

"The bathroom?"

Harry snorted, "Ha. The whole place is a dump. Heck, it's called The Can – go wherever you want."

"EXCUSE ME, No!" Gilly piped up louder than he had heard her speak yet. "We are a civilized group here, mate. Come with me to Lou."

She grabbed his hand and led him across the small clearing to a squat archway formed by doorless kitchen cabinets.

"Okay, this is Lou. One tunnel for the boys, that one for the girls. There's a toilet back in there… at least I *hope* there's one in yours – I've never been in there – and I don't plan on going, either." She wrinkled her nose.

"There's also a shower, sort of. But we need to conserve rain water. So we ration out the time in the showers. I think Dante has today. But do wash your hands, we are civilized."

She patted Monty's arm but then got a whiff of Monty. Having come a thousand miles under wet garbage gave him a bit of a ripe fragrance.

"On second thought, why don't you wash more than your hands. You can use my shower time today. Just conserve the water. You know, like you're camping." She leans closer and then jerks away, "but don't go easy on the soap."

Monty walked down a corridor made of crates, sheet metal and a hodgepodge of other materials. The hallway had an open ceiling and he could see the sun starting to arc across the mouth of The Can some thousand feet above his head.

He approached the back of the hall which ended in a heavily dented door of a porta-potty. A smiling skunk was tattooed on the door. A speech bubble had been drawn from the skunk's mouth where a message was written with an angry hand. It read: "BOYS only...NO girls. That means YOU Rachel!!"

Hovering above and slightly behind the door were two plastic kiddie pools. Belmont could see through the opaque bottoms of the pools. Sunlight danced off the waterline and reflected against the walls. Stretching upwards from the pools were tarps strung at angles and fastened by jump ropes and wires tied to heavier objects.

"Huh. They're capturing rainwater. Smart." Thought Belmont as he opened the bathroom door.

The small room behind the door glowed bluish from the sunlight coming through the pools above. There was a toilet seat in front of him with no lid. Belmont winced as he edged towards the seat and peeked down into the hole.

The hole formed a well that fell about four feet into the bubbling green-brown ooze that surrounded the fort. As Belmont watched, a MugSlug surfaced, rolled and sank back under the muck.

Monty shut the door behind him, which opened up a previously hidden small closet to the left.

As Belmont relieved himself he noted his tiny surroundings.

The closet was formed by tightly stacked plastic garbage cans, which helped to support the kiddie pools. An oversized shower head hung from a severely duct-taped garden hose in the center of one of the plastic pools. A small pull chain dangled next to the shower head.

The floor was a patchwork of linoleum pieces and bits of tile. A small chipped mirror was taped to a can facing the shower stall.

Two open plastic bins stood in the shower stall. One of the bins was overflowing with tiny plastic bottles of shampoo, conditioner, mouthwash, body lotion, shower gel, crème rinse, bath oils and other assorted mini-luxuries. Tiny wrapped bars of soap lay peppered among the bottles. Clearly all castaways from hotels and the like.

Belmont hung his soiled clothes on a rusted hook drilled into the garbage pail wall.

He selected a bottle of shower gel labeled "Red Oaks Resort Golf & Spa" and began to lather up.

The soap felt great and he was surprised he used the entire bottle just on his torso. He reached for a bottle of "Heaven-Lee Green-Tea Shampoo" and did the same with his hair.

He started to feel a bit like himself again as he scrubbed at the caked-in mud. He kneaded the shampoo into his hair and reached for the shower chain through tightly squeezed eyes…

A torrent of icy water dumped on Belmont with the force of a firehouse and took his breath away. Later, Rachel chided him that they were sure to be rescued now, since you were able to hear his high pitched scream all the way in Tokyo.

Peke

After a few days with the JYKs, he got to know the fort a little better. It was as if there were an endless number of nooks and crannies. He'd watch Apple seemingly disappear into one open barrel only to appear a few minutes later out of an empty drain pipe hidden on the other side of the clearing.

As for the clearing, for some reason they called it Glen. Not *the* Glen or *A* Glen. Just Glen, like a person. As in "They're all at Glen eating dinner" or "we're playing Putter-Putter at Glen in twenty minutes".

In fact most of the rooms and fixtures around the fort had names. Flush, Snore, Fridge, Magma. There was this tall tower of trash that reached higher than any other point in the Fort. In fact, it was the highest point in the vicinity.

Monty liked to go there and stare at the spectacular view. It became a quiet place that he would go to think. He would usually bring a partially used notepad and bits of crayon that he had found to take notes on the people he had met. He also started work drawing a map.

He knew this landscape, of course. He had seen his father's blueprints hundreds of times. He would watch as his father worried over this detail and that detail as he was designing this massive receptacle.

Belmont had left his favorite map back at home thousands of miles from here. But he had re-created a map from memory. He had one that he was particularly proud of. He thought it accurately showed the various quadrants and the water treatment lakes cutting through them all.

Of course with this vantage point, and his limited experience at the bottom of The Can, he was able to add details that were previously unknown to him.

He had a section showing MucLake, an octagon showing the location of the fort inside the lake and a small triangle representing Peke.

He showed the group over dinner one day, and they were all very interested, although Harrison pretended not to be.

The kids gave Belmont some advice on adding to the map and asked if he could use it to help map out the territory. Martin had been trying to do exactly that, but he didn't have the same perspective of the area – and his artistic skills were seriously lacking.

While they were offering comments on the map, Belmont had asked the kids about a tower of trash even taller than Peke. Gilly told Belmont it was called Morge Mountain, but they wouldn't say much more about it.

Whittling Arrows

Most of The JYKs had left to go "forage for food". Belmont had been left behind along with Dante, Martin and Magnus. And of course the ever-present Sparks. Dante was busying himself preparing some delicious smelling food over Magma. Magnus was on the other side of Glen, moving huge boulders of rubble to add to a wall that seemed to be shorter than the rest.

Martin was whittling a stick into a sharp arrow point.

"What's the arrow for?" Belmont inquired.

"We're going hunting tomorrow. Dante thought he saw a whole flock of Goozels on BioSide."

"A flock of what? You mean geese?"

"Nope. A Goozel. Big fat plumpy bird. Looks a bit like a goose and a bit like a turkey and whole bunch of dumb. Those eggs you were eating this morning, Goozel eggs. Also big, fat and plumpy. Have you ever had roast Goozel?"

"Um, no. I don't think so."

"Well, I haven't either. But that won't stop us from dining on some soon. Listen, my brother can make MugSlug taste like sweet potatoes, but that doesn't mean I don't get hungry for some real grub, you know what I mean?"

"Um, MugSlug…?"

"Not often. Only when we're desperate." Martin quickly added, sensing Monty's repulsion.

"*Más a menudo de lo que piensas*," mumbled Dante under his breath, as he swung a huge metal bucket of broth over Magma, suspended on a swiveling coat rack. The soup bubbled, and Monty fought back a burst of nausea.

"But, Goozels. Think of how delicious those would be. Maybe cooked with some onions and apples…"

Dante made a face and said, "*Por favor, déjame la cocina. Si eras el cocinero, quemarías una olla de agua.*"

"And we're getting pretty handy with these bows. Watch this," he stood up holding his new arrow. He grabbed a shoddy looking bow that seemed to be made out of a clothes hanger and a long strand of tied rubber bands.

He walked to the center of the clearing and pointed at a huge torn sign leaning against the wall of Fort. The sign was from an old billboard that said "…ARGET" and had a big red circle inside another red ring.

"Ready. Aim. Fire!" Martin let the arrow go. It shot wide of the target. It shot wide of the entire sign and thunked into an old ottoman that Magnus was carrying with one hand. He peered down at the arrow, and plucked it out staring curiously at the missile.

"Whoo-Hoo! Did you see that? It actually worked. I hit something. I've never got it to stick before! Those Goozels don't stand a chance."

Monty saw Magnus lift the arrow to his mouth and use it like a toothpick. Martin returned to Magma completely pleased with himself, and started to whittle another arrow.

Belmont had been meaning to ask someone about The Can and its inhabitants without causing conflict. Harrison's angry response to The Can and its developers had made Belmont nervous. But he chanced a question now.

"So how much do you know about this place?"

"What, The Can? Oh loads. You know, I don't want to brag or anything, but I used to study environmental sciences at school. I was good too. Best in the class, until I…" Martin's mood saddened and he paused. "Well… that's another story for another time. You asked about The Can, and let me tell you what I know."

The Can

"It's officially called the Global Waste and Hazardous Material Processing facility. GWAHMP for short. The engineers tried to give it a rather stoic sounding name of GWAHMP Canyon. However, it's become *un*affectionately nicknamed The Can.

"Have you ever heard of the Mariana Trench? It's the lowest point on the entire globe, deep deep deep under the Pacific Ocean. And how do you make the lowest area in the world lower? To start, you dig a well, and dump trash all over its face."

"Ellos no cavaron el pozo." Dante interrupted, coming back to Magma with an armful of potatoes.

"Okay, they didn't *dig* it. They made it. They built a ring of cement to the deepest part of this ocean trench, pumped all of the water out of it, collected the world's garbage – and dumped it in. We're at the bottom of that well… 35,000 feet below sea level.

"The walls of this wonderful facility angle all the way down from the surface of the ocean. And the walls aren't solid. They are honeycombed inside with a network of working tunnels and machinery that separate and sort the trash."

"There are seaports up there," he pointed to the rim of the Canyon thousands of feet up. "We call it TopDeck. That's how the trash gets here; by boat. Then it's dumped into these giant holes in the TopDeck where it's processed. You know, separated, sorted, decontaminated – kinda. And then it comes down through chutes in the walls…and *voila*, ends up here."

"Supposedly, the walls can also be lowered a bit so the ocean flows over the top and, um…*flushes* free floating garbage from the ocean into The Can… which supposedly gives it a rather 'toilet bowl' look – hence, the nickname The Can, is so fitting."

"That's the Pacific Garbage Patch they were trying to drain," added Belmont quietly.

"Yes. Yes, I think you're right." Martin responded, impressed that Belmont knew his history of environmental issues.

"They sliced this *beautiful* paradise into four sections – one for each brand of truly lovely refuse." Martin's pinky finger went up in an aristocratic way. "Specifically biodegradables, recyclables, hazardous materials and the last one for other flotsam and jetsam. There's also a sort of construction area. It may have been a base for workers, if they had to come down here. Although we've obviously never seen anyone down here. I'm not sure this place was built for humans…"

"I'm surprised it's not colder. The sun only seems to be available for a few hours. I'd think it was cold." Monty pondered.

"You'd think. But, The Can is near Guam, so it's not exactly a chilly spot. And, we're so far underwater, we're into the earth's mantle. That's why we get these magma bubbles…like our campfire here." Martin threw a handful of the wood shavings into Magma, which curled into tiny sprouts of fire.

"They use the lava to heat the lake, too. You saw the lake from Peke right?" he referenced the highest point of the fort over his shoulder. "At one end of the lake, the polluted water oozes in and is immediately boiled by volcanic heat. That's Sludge. Then the water filters through a few dams until it's relatively clean, eventually ending in Reservoir. We swim in it ya know."

"What? You swim down there?"

"Sure. Swim and skurf. It's amazing. There's this network of cables and motorized pulleys that crisscross the lake. I assume they were used to haul stuff back and forth across the water. We use these to ski behind. The winch operator runs on electricity from the lighting grid above." Martin pointed to the wire mesh that hung a hundred feet above the fort. "Those automatically go on and off every day at…well, we don't really know what times, but we say Supper in the evening."

"*Hablando de Cena, necesito tu ayuda para terminar esto a tiempo. Ve a lavar la lechuga y saca los platos del fregadero.*" Dante snapped at them.

"Well, that's pretty much all I got in this place. Oh yeah, and one more thing…it's inhabited by terrible monsters. Okay? Now, Dante wants us to help with dinner. Which do you want, lettuce or dishes?"

Monty was dumbstruck by this last comment. Monsters. There it was. Confirmation that what his dad said was true. The workers *had* been changed…into monsters!

Forage

"So Monty, ready to go foraging today?" Rachel asked.

Monty had woken up feeling well rested on his fourth morning in the fort. He was starting to feel a bit restless, so was glad for the offer.

"I, uh, guess so. How do we do it? Where do we get food from? Is some of the garbage safe?" he said around a mouthful of potatoes, and then pointed at his plate with his fork, " 'cause this is really good."

"Not garbage. First it's garbagy, then *not* garbagy. You'll see." Apple chirped.

A little foraging party was organized. Rachel, Dante and Martin held large empty sacks and heavily tattered gym bags. Belmont was given a one-strapped backpack. Harrison had a red gym bag slung across his chest.

"We'll see you later. Apple, don't leave the Fort," Apple was busy having a staring contest with Sparks over the tennis ball. "Magnus, make sure she doesn't leave the Fort."

Gilly waved, "Oh, she'll be Jake. We got eyes on her."

Apples pouted and stuck out her tongue at them.

"We always leave someone to guard the fort," said Rachel before she ducked into the tunnel that wound its way towards the exit.

"Yeah, and to keep Sparks company." Added Martin before following her.

"Why can't he come? Wouldn't he be a helpful guard dog?" Belmont asked Dante, who snort-chuckled at the suggestion.

"Sparks doesn't leave Fort," Gilly started.

"Yes he does!" Harry interrupted, coming to the dog's defense.

"Okay, barely. Sparks doesn't leave the *area*. He won't even leave for that stinky old ball. He'll stop every time at the gate."

The dog's ears went up at the word "ball" which released a slight static arc between them. But the ears went flat against his head at the word "gate".

"He's afraid…" she continued.

"He's not scared, just smart. Aren'tcha boy." Harry scratched the dog's rump but pulled back quickly as he received a slight shock. "And staticy!" He kicked the ball which sent the dog scrambling.

———

They all filed out and paused before the path over MucLake.

They followed a slightly different path to leave as they were going in the opposite direction from where they came in a few nights before. They used a similar number of hops and jumps to cross the lake of muck, but there weren't as many monkey bars. There was a point where they climbed a rickety ladder and slid down the hollow insides of an old metal row boat. But it was relatively easy going. Belmont was quietly thankful since his arms ached for a few days after coming in.

As they left MucLake behind, the amount of trash and hills of garbage thinned out a bit. Here and there Belmont saw a patch of brown tangled grass or a thorny leafless bush.

"Things grow down here?"

"Sure do. We have dirt, we have water, we even have sunlight – maybe not as long as everybody else…" She waved her arm upwards at the huge ever-present walls towering above them, "but we get enough."

"Yeah, but where do you get the plants?"

"People throw them away." Martin chimed in, "Well, not the plants exactly. But the seeds."

"Really, Why?"

"Why?? You like apples right… but you don't eat the core, right? Well neither does anybody in the world," Harrison snapped.

"*Magnus come todo lo que está delante de su gran cabeza*," Dante said to the group, even though only his brother could understand him.

"Well, okay maybe him, but nobody else does.... So they get tossed. They get processed and they end up here. Then nature takes over. They land in dirt – heavily fertilized with the apple cores of millions of other apple-eaters, and well, there you go."

As he finished his bit, they rounded a hill in their path and the scene below them was fantastic. It was a narrow valley full of lush vegetation, probably about a mile long and about a half a mile wide. The slopes of the Valley were covered in fruit bearing trees, and they fell slowly down towards a meandering stream. The banks of the creek were spotted with corn and vegetable patches. They were on a small ledge that overlooked the valley, and seemed to be ripe with herbs and lemon grasses... it was beautiful.

"OH, how beautiful."

Rachel, shaking her hair out and massaging her shoulders, turned suddenly with a wink and said, "Why thank you, but keep your eyes on the road."

"No, not you...the view. I mean, *Not*, not you. I mean you are, but...I mean the field is beautiful."

Rachel turned towards the view concealing a smile while Belmont blushed deep red.

"We rest here for a bit."

They all sat down on upturned buckets and random objects – it was apparent the group had stopped here before. They passed around a heavily duct-taped plastic jug full of water and filled a few plastic cups.

"There's not much garbage here."

Martin unfolded a worn piece of cardboard. On one side was a smiling toothpaste dad, and the other was a badly drawn map.

"You see, the landfill on this side comes down from the southern wall. The trash builds up considerably towards the wall, and then mostly slopes downward from there. Fort is about halfway across Flotsam between here and the wall."

"That's GlumpBog we are walking towards. GlumpBog kind of hugs that boiling mass of..." he pointed to a huge bubbling brown pond of goo that pooled around the eastern edge of the canyon wall.

"Cacka," Dante smiled.

"Yeah, Cacka. That Cacka – that's Sludge. It is mostly sewage pumped in to be boiled from underneath."

"From Magma, we assume." Rachel added.

"The boiled sludge then rolls down those rapids over there, cooling as it goes, and forms GlumpBog."

"From there, the sediment settles, and slightly cleaner water passes into that second set of rapids and treatment machinery there," Martin gestured to a host of small arching bridges over some rapids and short water chutes.

"Then the mostly clean water dumps into Reservoir. We assume that was the deepest part of the Mariana Trench. It's a deep saltwater lake that is thousands of years old."

Belmont knew much of this already, but was fascinated with the lush landscape below them. He couldn't have imagined that the massive garbage dump his fathers company had built would hold such lush vegetation.

"But what about the plants? All that came from garbage??"

"Yes. That section is BioSide. That is where all of the biodegradable garbage is dumped. So your lawn clippings, leaves and yard waste. Your pineapple tops and apple cores and peach pits and…"

"Fish heads…"

"French fry oil…"

"Granos de café."

"Right," Martin continued. "And on this side is the stuff of auto parts, crates, furniture, construction debris and stuff like that."

Belmont continued thoughtfully, "Refuse Area South. Those non-biodegradable solid materials that are neither easily recycled nor recognized to pose serious environmental or health concerns. Refuse Area South…"

This was met with silence. When Belmont looked up from his water, they were all staring at him with their mouths open.

Rachel broke the silence "Um…I Thought you just got here. What's with the super-knowledge all of a sudden?"

"Yeah, what is with the tech-know?"

"*¿Has trabajado aquí?*" Dante asked, with his eyebrows up.

"Yeah… did you work here or something??"

"Um, No. Well, not exactly. But, um…"

"Out with it!" Harrison snapped.

"Well, my dad kinda built this place." He stammered nervously.

"Built this place?? What the heck does that mean?" Rachel snarled.

"Yeah. Your dad couldn't have built this. Obviously, this gargantuan structure required about, um, seventy-two hundred laborers," Martin responded quizzically, seeming to ponder the man hours required to build the miles-tall walls. "Yeah, working double shifts would probably take about three years."

"It took almost four years, actually – many on triple shifts. And that's just the construction. Never mind the planning, design, funding…and a few failed attempts …"

When no one responded, Belmont mistook their silence as impressed disbelief.

"Yes. It required some of the best minds in the world working on this. My dad had to meet with all kinds of World Leaders – presidents and kings. And I came up with the idea…"

Rachel, who had been quietly staring open mouthed at him strode over to Belmont and stabbed her pointer finger into his chest, hard.

"You mean to tell me. You mean to tell *us that* your old man. That *you* and your old man came up with the idea to build a crapper in the middle of nowhere and then all the shiny happy people in the world would send the most vile disgusting garbage to sit and rot, and with it the unwanted rats and cats and volefants to disappear, forever?! And never be able to escape no matter how hard we try??!" she was yelling and turning a bright red.

Belmont shrank away from her and was afraid she might punch him in the nose.

"Wait wait, Rachel, don't kill him." Harrison had been contemplating the situation but stepped between them. "No seriously. This might be good. Yeah. We can use this information – or his information. Think about it. Who would know more about this place than the guy who built it?"

"I, ah, i, um…" Belmont gulped.

"You think I give a *sugar* if he knew how to fly out of here on a magic piece of cardboard? He built the place that we have been stuck in for…god knows how long."

"I didn't, well, I um…" Belmont moaned.

"But seriously, once you get over that fact, maybe he knows a way out. Or has an idea how to get into the tunnels." Martin said.

"The tunnels." Harrison said to himself.

"Yeah, the tunnels. He'd know the way." Martin said again.

"Excuse me... I was, um..." Belmont whispered.

"And what, we have him draw a map and we just climb right on up out of here. Just like that??"

"Wait, excuse me..."

"Yeah, just like that. I mean, who would know more about the tunnels than the guy who designed them?" Harrison said to a still fuming Rachel.

"Excuse me," Belmont squeaked.

"What??" they all asked in unison, staring at him.

"Um," clearing his throat. "I was, um, only two years old."

They all stared blankly at him with their mouths agape. Harrison finally broke the silence.

"Nevermind. Kill him."

Gator?

They had left base camp about an hour earlier. They were wandering slowly down the gentle slope towards the muddy river. There was a path just wide enough for two people to walk side-by-side, unless you wanted to walk in mud that hid broken glass and bottle caps.

Rachel hadn't killed Monty. But she did shove him. And no one had talked to him for the past hour at least. Well, except Dante, who kept chattering to him in Spanish. But Monty couldn't understand a word.

Belmont had tried to slide next to Rachel and strike up conversation. But she wasn't interested and instead Dante happily continued to chat uninterrupted.

Periodically, Dante would stop and leave the trail and, using half a length of garden rake, pick up some particularly gross garbage and plop it into a plastic sack he was carrying.

While Belmont didn't understand a word, he was glad for some company. And the walk had been pleasant enough. As this place goes, the view was sort of nice, and the tall piles of trash had dwindled considerably.

As they approached the Bog, Belmont noticed a rickety jumble of boards that bridged the water. They stopped in a dry creek bed that ended at the brownish-greenish water of the Bog. Air would burble to the surface, the bubble would grow oily and fat and then burst with a glumpy "pop".

"Rest here again so we can gather and be back here in one hour."

The mood seemed to lighten a bit and everyone seemed a little excited. Martin came over to Monty and put his hand on his shoulder. Monty turned around.

"Sorry for the radio-silence there. It's just that, well, we're stuck here and it hasn't been easy. Especially on Rachel. But we'll get over it. In fact I want to know how you came up with this idea. I mean, it's an amazing feat of mankind – even if I'm trapped here forever," he finished with a smile, joking good naturedly.

"Thanks Martin. Sorry if I upset the group and got everyone mad at me."

Martin filled Monty's empty cup with water, "Hey, forget it. In fact, you've impressed Dante. He thinks you're the best. He finally thinks someone here is almost as smart as he is."

"That's cool, I guess. Hey. He's a nice guy and everything, but why does he keep picking up garbage? And I mean *really* yucky garbage. I saw him pick up a diaper – a *used* diaper, if you know what I mean. I thought we were getting food, not...eeek!"

Belmont dropped his water and shook his hand. "Yikes! There's a lizard on my hand. Get off!" He shook it again, as a small reptile gripped Monty's middle finger. It was the size of a magic marker, but resembled a much larger animal.

"Is this a little alligator! Hey, get off of me."

"It's not an alligator." Martin said.

"Yes it is, look," he stopped waggling his hand because it wasn't accomplishing anything and Belmont's curiosity got the best of him, "Look at its mouth. It's no ordinary lizard – It's totally a little alligator."

"Nope. It's a crocodile. Actually, a crocodilly." Martin offered, "Alligators have rounded snouts, and downward turned teeth. And they usually have darker spots under each eye...and they are different sizes."

He was no longer grossed out by the animal, and started to study him. "I don't know. This guy seems to look like an alligator to me."

Meanwhile, a dark shadow fell onto the shoreline and started growing behind Belmont. There began a low rumble, almost like a revving engine. Belmont stood completely engrossed in the little creature. "I see the teeth, and I guess they aren't all 'down turned'. Well yeah, and obviously the 'size difference', but this guy is so small."

"Trust me, that's a crocodilly. The size difference to an alligator is, um, considerable." Martin said, as he looked up and started to back away from Monty.

The shadow had grown and was starting to block out the light, and the noise was so loud that it couldn't be ignored.

"Okay, I guess this is a crocodile..." Belmont trailed off as he was overtaken by a terrible smell. He slowly turned around and came face to face with the enormous open maw of a huge monstrous lizard.

The beast was as big as a car. Bigger. A large van. Its mouth alone was twice longer than Belmont was tall.

The jagged teeth were all pointed downward – directly at Belmont. Its jaws opened wider and a dank, rotten smell flooded over Belmont. Its mouth was widening and widening as the rumbling got louder. Belmont stood staring directly into a wet jagged cave of a gigantic alligator's mouth.

Belmont vaguely heard yelling behind him.

"...back. Get Back!!"

He stumbled backwards a bit and tripped over an empty bottle. He landed hard on his bum and stared upwards into the dripping mouth. The beast was almost on top of him. Its claws dug into the creek bed and pulled its massive chest forward an inch.

Dante was suddenly beside him turning in a circle while swinging the garbage bag he had been holding around with him. He let the sack go and it flew into the beast's mouth.

The monster snapped its jaws closed with the sound of a head-on collision. It hoisted its enormous snout into the air, whipping river muck and mud all over Belmont. From his position, he was able to see the massive throat open and swallow the entire bag in one gulp before slinking back into the bog. Its huge mass slowly sank below the surface like a rock in a bucket of pudding.

Finally, the eyes and terrible snout disappeared under the muck with a final burst of a bubble, and all was quiet.

Belmont sat up and turned to the group. They were all hoisting their bags onto their shoulders and getting ready to cross the bridge as if nothing had happened. Finally Rachel saw Belmont covered from head to toe in river muck and tried to suppress a giggle. Then Dante saw what she was laughing at and started to laugh as well. Harry joined in, as did Martin. Everybody was laughing at the mud drenched boy that stood dripping in front of them.

"See – that was an alligator." Martin said. "Well, actually a giganticgator."

Rachel was sort of smiling, "Don't worry, they don't eat people. Not usually anyway. Not when you have such lovely garbage to feed them. Although, with the way you look, she may make an exception. Come on, let's get you washed off over here."

Belmont held up his finger with the crocodilly still firmly grasping his forefinger.

"I definitely see the differences, and you're much less dangerous, aren't you?"

As if on cue, the reptile responded by biting his thumb.

BioSide

The air felt different as soon as they crossed the river. It wasn't so metallic, not as rusty smelling as the refuse side. And it was damper. Maybe not damp, but dank. Dank and ripe.

"It smells a bit, um, riper over here," Monty said to no one in particular.

"That's the Bio," said Martin. "You see, this is some of the most fertile soil in this place.

Rachel reached down to grab a handful of moist dirt and let it crumble between her fingers. Small bits of orange peels could be seen among dark sticky mud. "It might be some of the most fertile soil in the world."

"What are you farmers?" He asked.

"Hmm, more like gatherers…" she wondered aloud as they crested the top of the hill and approached the beautiful landscape below.

It was beautiful. The sun sparkled on top of corn stalks and shone on red apples filling a grove of trees. A large watermelon was lying directly in the path at their feet.

"All of this is from Unpopped popcorn kernels and apple seeds?"

"Hard to believe, but true. And it's the only reason we've been able to survive down here." Martin said.

Dante had foraged up ahead and was returning with a bag of root vegetables. A few others had bags full of apples and carrots. Belmont wandered around taking in the sights and looking at the lush fruit and vegetables growing in patches on the valley floor. He helped gather a few as Rachel was whistling and motioning for the group to get together. Rachel picked up the watermelon and they started loading them into a large canvas sack.

"Put them all in here. Rooties on bottom because they won't get crushed. This baby on top," she placed the watermelon on the mound of veggies. "That's it. Let's go," and she turned around to leave.

"What. Why are we leaving so quickly? Why don't we stay longer? We could eat here.... In fact, why don't you just live on this side?" Belmont asked curiously.

"It's not exactly safe after dark," said Rachel. But she wouldn't say anything more.

Morges

Martin and Dante were swinging a large canvas bag between them. They were leading the procession back to the fort by cutting across a rise in the landscape before taking the path down to the bridge over the Giganticgator's lair.

The bag was overflowing with apples, peaches, potatoes and one very large melon. There were also some odd garlic-flowery things, blue fennel bulbs and a strange nut the exact size and shape of a banana.

Harry followed the twins, he had been the least forgiving for Monty's part in manufacturing the Canyon. He was grumbling to himself about why anyone would make this "blankety-blank" hole in the ocean.

Rachel was next in line and behind her, at a healthy distance, was Belmont.

"This isn't exactly fair." Thought Monty. Although the mood had lightened a bit since Monty had confessed to his family's involvement in constructing The Can, he was still getting the cold shoulder from the group. "Obviously, I didn't have much to do with this facility. And my dad surely didn't build it to trap kids."

Also, he had participated significantly in the gathering of potatoes and turnips to help fill the bag. And didn't Rachael use his back as a step ladder to reach that Bonderfus Bean, or whatever it was called?

Monty kicked at a loose spring in the path. Then he watched it bounce a short distance down the rise that they were currently marching across. Monty's eyes wandered upwards towards the lake in the far distance.

He saw motion at the bottom of the hill about two hundred yards below. Climbing up a pile of destroyed cabinetry and drywall was an ape-like creature. It was too far away to make out any details, but it seemed human sized.

"Hey Rachel," Belmont said.

"Shush!" she replied, "I'm still not talking to you!"

"Okay. Fine. But I have a question."

"Make it quick," she snapped.

"Okay, what are those?" Belmont asked, pointing down the hill.

"Quiet. Not so loud, we don't want to be heard by…"

She cut her response short, and immediately fell to the ground.

"Belmont. Down!" She hissed loudly.

Belmont was slow to hit the ground so Rachel motioned forcefully with her hand. He got down to his knees and slowly laid on his belly.

"Harry, Martin… Dante, stop!" Rachel hissed to the group, just loud enough for them to hear.

Martin and Dante stopped short. Harry was a step slower and struggled to stop before bumping into the canvas bag. The melon teetered on top of the canvas bag and threatened to roll off.

All three of them turned to look at Rachel on the ground, and then they followed her gaze downhill.

They immediately fell to the ground and put their heads down.

"¡Son ellos!" Dante said.

"Stay down. Keep quiet," hissed Rachel. "Oh no, the melon. Watch the melon!" And she stared pointedly at the bag.

The twin's sudden movement freed the melon from the canvas bag, and it rolled slowly out. Fortunately, it leaned against a rusty bolt on the ground and stopped.

Everyone breathed lighter.

"But what are they?" Asked Belmont again.

Rachel quickly army-crawled backwards to be closer to Belmont. She leaned in towards his ear.

"They are Morges. And they are terrible. They will eat you if they see you…" Then she recoiled at the still drying muck in his hair "…Unless maybe they smell you first! Now quiet!"

"Morges…?!"

Rachel put her finger up to her lips harshly, and Belmont cut himself off.

There were two creatures now, both climbing over the construction waste. They were loping along, lifting one arm and swinging forward on their stubby legs. They reached the top of the massive pile, then started to move down out of sight.

From this distance, Belmont couldn't see the beasts well. He hoped it was the same from their vantage point.

The creatures disappeared completely from view and the group relaxed a bit.

Harry breathed out as if he were holding his breath. Rachel put her forehead down onto the path.

Martin and Dante both started to get up slowly, but the gravel shifted underneath one of them and the melon rocked slowly towards the slope of the hill.

Everyone watched in slow motion and then both Martin and Dante lunged at the fruit simultaneously. They collided awkwardly and both fell short. The melon rolled slowly out of reach and hung on the edge of the hill for a moment.

It bounced gently once over a short edge and disappeared for half a moment out of sight. Martin quickly climbed towards them both and pushed their heads in the sand. At that immediate moment, a dark shape appeared over the construction debris, and stared in their direction.

It was the head of one of the Morges looking for the source of the noise.

The melon had disappeared from view for a moment, but came rolling faster down the slight incline.

The head remained motionless as the melon dropped down towards the debris pile. The group held their breath collectively, hoping they were sufficiently hidden from view at the top of this hill. They peeked through splayed fingers or from behind tangles of wires.

Suddenly, there was tremendous action below.

The melon bounded one last time as it reached the bottom of the hill. At that moment, the animal pounced like a panther. Its arms and legs were splayed out and each limb ended in terrible claws. Blinding fangs could be seen in the beast's mouth, even from their distance.

The melon didn't stand a chance.

The animal's mouth was open wide and slammed shut on the fruit in midair. The melon exploded in a wet and gruesome mess, peppering the hillside and debris with blood-red juice and chunks of melon flesh.

The Morge landed chewing the melon rind while looking around aggressively for any further action. Then it looked up the hill where the melon had come from.

If possible, the group flattened themselves even more onto the dirt path. As he squeezed the ground, Belmont felt a sharp pain in his cheek from a shard of glass.

The beast looked around a few more minutes and then leapt quickly onto the debris pile and swung out of view.

The group laid hugging the ground, not daring to make a noise for a long period of time.

The sun set behind the lip of The Can and they were plunged into shadows. Slowly, the light grid above them began to hum and illuminate the hillside. Even then they remained stock still.

Only when the Crackets started to chirp, did Rachel finally break the silence. She lifted her head, her face framed by a ring of dust and dirt, and said, "That was a Morge. And as I said: They. Are. Terrible."

The Vote

"**A**nother Morge sighting," Harry announced as they crawled into Glen from the outside. "Just over MucCreek; and it was even before ShadowSet."

Gilly and Apple were playing with a tangle of yarn and Magnus was hefting a block of twisted steel onto another block. He paused in mid-motion with the block over his head.

"Could someone please tell me what those were," said Belmont for the upteenth time. "Don't I deserve to know?"

"Deserve? Deserve?! You think you deserve anything from us?" Harry barked at Belmont. Then he said to the group, "And in other news, Belmont and his daddy made GWAHMP Canyon! Yep. They are the ones who dug this hole in the ocean, dumped in the trash, collected all of the world's most dangerous NewBeasts and let them live here like some sort of twisted zoo. He's responsible for us being stuck here!"

"*Eso puede estar yendo un poco lejos,*" Dante said.

"Yeah, I don't know if he's responsible, as such…" added Martin.

"Let's take it easy," said Rachel. She had lightened up on Belmont since he was the first to spot the Morges.

"Easy?! We may never get out of here again. We may never see our families and friends again because this little turd-wink had a good idea to dig a well and leave it unsupervised in the middle of the blam-danked ocean!" Harry paused and then stared at Monty.

"I don't think I should 'take it easy'. I think Belmont should go fend for himself…out there." He ended by pointing firmly over the fort's trash walls.

Belmont looked around for support, but no one met his gaze. They were looking at their shoes or around, but not at him. Only Harry glared into his eyes.

"Fine. Okay," Monty sighed, "if that's what you want. But first hear me out. I've had a rough go of it too. You think I haven't? I'm stuck down here just like you. I miss my dad. I miss my friends. I especially miss my one-mattress bed."

Dante chuckled.

"But you know why this place was built? Because the pollution was terrible. It was killing wildlife. The forests, the trees, the oceans. Diseases that had been eradicated were coming back like mini-plagues. People were dying. Parents and kids. My mom…" Belmont choked on his words as a sob interrupted his speech. He took a breath, composed himself and started again slowly.

"I understand this place sucks. I understand this place is dangerous. I don't like it either." He sighed. "It was nice to be included in your group for a while. You let me in and you fed me. And clothed me – although you have terrible style." He pulled at his red Christmas pajama top.

This time Martin and Gilly joined Dante in a chuckle.

"But I understand if you want me gone for my part in creating…this," he held up his arms to encompass the entire facility. He stood for a moment, and then put his arms down. "I'll go get my things."

Then he left head bent, walking into the corridor that led to Snore.

The group was silent for a few minutes after he left. Some dug their toes into the dirt, Gilly twisted at a lock of her hair.

"*Eso no me hizo sentir bien,*" Dante said, breaking the silence.

"I agree. I feel terrible. Did he say his *mom* died from pollution sickness?" Martin added.

"Belmonty is nicey-nice. BunnyBunBuns wants him to stay," Apple chirped.

Rachel held her hand up to get everyone's attention, "Guys, I know we're angry. And I know we are very surprised at the news that Belmont and his family were involved in this…trap. But, let's be honest. If we weren't down here, we'd probably think it was a good idea too. Right? I mean, we remember what it was like UpTop. The trash in our neighborhoods. The polluted air and streets. We remember how polluted the lakes and oceans were. We couldn't even *swim* without worrying about getting tangled in some trash…"

"You don't swim, remember?" Harry huffed.

"That's not the point. What does matter is that something did need to be done. And his family was trying to solve a bigger problem. Possibly saving the rest of the planet, even though we got caught in the middle."

A few nods around the group.

"So what do you say? Who's for letting Belmont stay?" She raised her hand higher.

Apple raised her hand, and put BunBun's paw in the air.

Magnus dropped the brick with a loud thud, and put his huge arm up. This was followed by Dante, then Gilly then Martin.

Finally, Harrison said begrudgingly, "Fine. He stays. But only because he'd probably get killed out there otherwise." He put up his hand.

Sparks came out of a hole he was digging, and shook himself off of dust. Then, seeing the group with their hands up, sat on his haunches and pawed at the air.

When Belmont returned with his backpack and original clothes on, the group was smiling eagerly at him.

Rachel started, "Monty, we get it. Your dad didn't do this on purpose, and we probably can't blame him… Or you… Completely."

"*Queremos que te quedes*," said Dante.

"We voted that you should stay. And we're sorry if we were mean. Well, if *they* were mean," said Gilly.

"Yay. Belmonty stay-stays. Let's celebrate. Can we DrumDrum?" Apple chimed in.

At that, Harrison perked up. "You are right. We'll celebrate. Tonight we Drum!"

Drum Circle

They took their now familiar places around Magma, as it burped orange bubbles of molten heat through a thin crust of cooling rock.

Dante was threading potatoes on a sharp wire and hung them over the smoldering pit. A wonderful smell of garlic and rosemary filled the air as Gilly picked up her guitar.

She strummed a few notes on the remaining strings on the neck, and hummed a lovely matching note. Unlike the last few nights, the others pulled various instruments seemingly out of nowhere.

"*Nosotros no hemos hecho esto en un tiempo*," said Dante.

"Yeah, this is a nice occasion. The Drum Circle. Last time we did this, we were going hunting the next day," replied Martin.

"Hmm, and so, tomorrow, hunt we will," said Harry with his best Yoda impression.

"What? Really? Awesome! This is just awesome. I've been working on the arrows and my bow skills have gotten *really* good. Ask Monty. I hit something yesterday. It was so great. Ah – I'm going to dream about that shot." Martin stared dreamily at the ARGET sign he had never hit.

Magnus and Monty looked at each other with raised eyebrows. They both shrugged and Magnus went back to fiddling with his instrument.

"We have it on good intel," Harry winked at Dante, who beamed, "that suggests the ever elusive Goozel flock is in the Wallside Fen. And we are going to get us some chicken!" Harry hoisted a chipped wooden spoon in the air for effect "…well, Goozel-meat anyway." He brought the spoon down onto a cookpot top with a shattering gong.

Apple started to shake her two soup cans fixed to the end of sticks as homemade maracas. Martin had a heavily duct-taped bongo and Magnus held a dented bucket and long rusty wrench they both started to pound in unison.

Martin produced a whistle from a chain around his neck and blew a shrill note. Immediately, the others started to bang, clang, strum, blow or shake their various instruments. It was a terrible cacophony of sound…but as they continued to bang away, the sounds fell into a sort of rhythm. It wasn't quite music; more of a tribal chant, but Monty could feel it in his chest, echoing his heartbeat.

Rachel handed Belmont a piece of PVC piping with holes down the front. Someone had taped a mouthpiece to it. When Belmont blew it, it sounded a bit like a clarinet and a lot like a duck. He smiled over the noise, and blew in short rhythmic bursts.

Apple was the first to stand up with her handmade maracas and started to shimmy in a circle around Magma. Gilly stood with a little "Whoop" and followed Apple, strumming her guitar loudly. Behind her came giant Magnus, making his dented bucket look (and sound) like a cowbell in his enormous hands.

Soon everyone was march-dancing around Magma, shouting at the dark haloed moon far above.

Monty, having gone from feeling like an outcast – lonely and alone, now started to feel part of something. He felt almost welcome. He had a sudden urge and howled loudly at the sky above. Harry laughed and joined him. Soon all of the JYKs were yipping and howling along with the music rhythm.

As their collective yowl faded, a longer howl lingered. There on an outcrop of rubble stood Sparks, glowing faintly blue as he joined in the ruckus.

Goozels

"So much excitement over this little adventure this morning. So again, what are we hunting?" Monty asked Gilly.

Magnus and Apple had stayed back at the fort. The rest of the JYKs were walking down a grassy path that led through the BioSide. They were closer to The Can's wall than Monty had yet been.

"Goozels. Dante saw a flock out here. They're like big cute geese but, um, maybe not as smart," she responded.

"They are dumber than bowling pins. You can go right up to them and bonk them in the head. And they taste awesome. Well, we *think* they taste awesome. We've never really caught one."

"If they're so dumb and slow, why haven't you caught one yet?"

"Well, we only recently discovered them in the first place. They're really good at camouflaging themselves. Their feathers look exactly like this grass." Martin swiped at the waist high prairie grass with his bow. "So you don't really see them until you're on top of them."

"*Magnus prácticamente pisó uno mientras estábamos forjando para el ajo hace unas noches.*" Dante chimed in.

"Yeah. For all his size, Magnus jumped about three feet in the air when he spooked it up. He thought he stumbled on a baby Morge or something. Ever since then, we've been watching for them. Dante believes he saw them grazing out here somewhere."

"*Estoy seguro de que los vi.*" Dante insisted.

"So how do we plan on catching them?" Belmont asked. "And are they *dangerous?*" he added, tentatively.

"We smack 'em in the head," Harry held up a tennis racket with a few strings missing, "and no, they're not dangerous. They're plump and delicious. I think."

"They're not dangerous, as such." Martin said, pondering. "But, there is something weird about them. I can't exactly remember what it is. Something about aging backwards or something…. But that sounds stupid. I mean they'd have to be hatched from a giant egg, and that can't be. We've found nests before and harvested their eggs. They are big as baseballs, but much tastier."

———

Harry held up his fist in a flexed arm way; stony looks to his right and to his left. He was gripping his tennis racket like a club. "Hold," he hissed at Rachel – who promptly stuck her tongue out at him.

But she did stop, despite herself. They all peered over a rotting little couch at the clearing of grass and wildflowers ahead.

Among the clover-berries and wild-onions were a handful of grazing birds. They resembled geese, but much fatter and with a short stumpy neck. Their wings stuck out at right angles from the sides, instead of folding up gracefully like a normal bird. And their feathers were the same color and shape of the tawny prairie grass that covered the fen. They stuck up from their backs like quills on a porcupine.

And they were big. Much bigger than a goose. About the size of an overstuffed laundry bag.

Harry gave them a steely look, and pointed two fingers at his eyes and then two fingers at everybody else's eyes.

Rachel hissed back, "Yeah, so we all have eyes, big deal!"

Belmont nodded eagerly and said, "Yes we do. She's right, we do."

Harry scowled and Belmont added, "I mean, you're right too, yeah you are right too. We have eyes." He smiled pitifully.

Harry whispered loudly, "No you dorks, that means 'watch me'."

"Okay. I got it."

Rachel was not as forgiving and added, "Why didn't you just say so?"

"Because, I'm trying to be quiet you knucklehead!"

"Well you're not being quiet now."

"That's because you're making me yell!" He yelled.

"*¡Los dos tienen que estar callados!*" Dante hissed, gesturing towards the birds.

Martin added, "Um, could you be quieter, the birds just looked this way."

Harry breathed slowly through his nose. "Okay listen, let's circle around them. Monty and Dante that way, Rachel and Gilly that way and Martin and me stay here."

"What, the girls can't play with the big boys?" Rachel snorted.

"No, I need you over there, and I need us to partly surround them. Monty and Dante will charge them while making noise, and we'll have them surrounded. When they run, they'll run into our hands. Got it?"

The crew turned and looked at the Goozels one last time before executing Harry's plan.

Crouching, each team circled the flock, staying out of sight as much as possible. Belmont and Dante were to circle to the left, and get directly on the opposite side of the clearing. Then they were going to jump up and rush the birds. Anticipating that they would scare easily and run in the direction of Harry.

Martin, being armed with his (not very accurate) bow, would wait until the last minute and shoot the birds.

Belmont and Dante got to their point across the little fen, and peeked out from a pile of crates. The clearing was about half the size of a soccer field and elliptical in shape. They were at the long end of the clearing and they could see most of their comrades partly around the circle.

"Okay, we'll shake these bottles full of nuts and bolts as we rush them. Once they get running, let's lag behind so we don't accidentally catch an arrow. Even though I doubt Martin could hit us from two feet away."

Dante nodded and held up five fingers…

"*Cinco, cuatro, tres, dos, uno – vamos!*"

Belmont and Dante jumped up and waved their arms wildly and shouted.

"Charge!!"

"*¡Ataque!*"

They rushed, yelling, through the tall onion stalks and shook the bottles for effect. The squat birds looked up and stared dumbly at the oncoming noisemakers, without as much as a twitch.

Dante and Belmont ran most of the distance to the birds, without seeing them move an inch.

Dante came up short a few steps before Belmont did. They both dropped their arms and stopped shaking the bottles to stare at the birds. Six pairs of flat, blank eyes blinked at the two boys unphased. One finished chewing and belched loudly.

"Well I guess they don't frighten easily…"

But then the boys saw them. Little chicks. About two dozen fluffy little white and yellow feathered chicks all napping cuddly-cue in a cozy feather nest.

Belmont said, "There are babies here!"

From across the field they heard Gilly say, "Awww"

"We can't kill them while they're protecting their babies. Not that they're doing a great job of it, but still."

Dante nodded. "*Si*"

"Hey Harry, there are chicks here. We can't kill these."

There was a curse and a loud shout from across the field.

"What did you say Martin?" Belmont asked loudly. "What? No it doesn't matter. See they're not scared, look." Belmont rattled his bottle again, and made a Boogaloo noise. "See, they won't run or do anything." He shook his hand-made rattle one last time.

Dante tossed his bottle gently at a particularly plump one, and hit it in the butt. The bird literally honked. Not like a goose exactly, more like a clown's horn.

"Oh shoot, look we woke the chicks up." Two dozen puffy, yellow, little fuzz-balls blinked their pale pink eyes, yawned and started peep-peep-peeping.

Another "Awwww" from Gilly across the clearing.

"Aw jeez. We can't eat these cute little guys. Just look at them. They're sooooo so cute…. Hey, maybe we can take them home with us and raise them as chickens?" Belmont crouched down to get a closer look and held out a finger to the nest.

At that movement, the Goozlings slowly turned their tiny little beaks towards the sound of Belmont in one coordinated motion.

"Hey, look at the little beaks. Are those... Teeth?" The tiny little chicks' gaze narrowed angrily. The pink eyes stared menacingly at the two children in the middle of the field.

"Um...Nice little chickie chicks...?" And then shouting to the rest of the group, "Hey, ah, these guys seem a little mad." One nipped at the outstretched finger. "Hey. He tried to bite me." Then louder to the group, "Hey, this one tried to bite me."

"Monty!" It was Martin's voice from across the field. He was using a bottomless cup as a megaphone. "I just remembered what I had forgotten before. You need to run. Run exactly now!!"

Suddenly the chicks collectively open their sharp beaks and let out an awful screech...

...And then they *charged*...

Belmont quickly looked at Dante, but he was already gone, running frantically away from the birds. He was running across the shorter end of the field, towards Gilly and Rachel.

Belmont backed up quickly and stumbled. He recovered and scrambled to his feet. The fastest of the chicks caught up with Belmont. It ran with its tiny little feet, flapped with its tiny little wings, rose up and opened its tiny little beak and sunk its *not so tiny little* teeth into Belmont's nose. "YOWWW!"

Belmont found himself eyeball to pink-eyeball with the cutest little fuzzball assassin that has ever been. The bird growled and shook its head like a dog with a sock.

Belmont screamed and ran.

The bird held on, shedding downy feathers as Belmont's long legs carried him past Dante. It positioned its little feet for leverage on the bridge of Belmont's nose and started to pull. He smacked at his face and knocked the bird off.

"¡Terrible pajarito!"

He saw out of the corner of his eye the yellow puff of aggression snap shut on Dante's wrist.

"Yow!" He screamed, and swatted the bird away, "¡Terrible pajarito!" Another chick had apparently caught up and was right there to replace the first blood thirsty little cotton ball.

"Hey D, these things bite.... And they hurt! A LOT!"

Dante's look didn't need translating.

They reached the edge of the clearing and Rachel and Gilly quickly scattered. They angled to the original hiding couch. Harry was waving them off to the other direction, while Martin unsheathed his bow.

The crew ran past them in a straight line; first Gilly, then Rachel, then Belmont followed by Dante. Belmont was being nipped in the butt while another kept snapping at his ears. Dante had a bird firmly on his head gnawing out tufts of hair and spitting it into the wind as he ran. A small angry flock followed closely behind and was gaining on them.

Martin and Harry steadied themselves for the attack as a dozen more yellow puffs, each the size of an apple, swarmed towards them.

A chick flew up snapping loudly in mid air, almost biting Harry's arm. It made another attempt and sunk its teeth into his hand. He screamed in pain. Another one landed at his other arm but this time he was quicker. He swatted it down with his racket making a loud *boing*.

You could hear Gilly's disapproving "Aww, don't hurt it" even as she ran like crazy from the assault.

"Are you kidding me, these things are trying to eat us! I'm gonna give them something to fear!"

For all of his big talk, Harry waved the racket around in a circle swinging at everything and hitting nothing. Two more puffballs attached themselves to each of his shoulders and started to nip his earlobes. He reached up instinctively and ripped them off the shoulders and flung them into the wind. Surprisingly, the birds rolled in the air, flapped their little wings and dive-bombed directly back at him.

"Fuzzy Duck! These things are vampires!" He chucked the racket at the flock and ran wildly.

Martin's bow went off unexpectedly with a sad little *twung*; the arrow fell harmlessly in between three evil cotton balls. They looked at the arrow quivering in the dirt and then swarmed Martin's head.

"ARRGH!" He jumped on the couch and rolled to get the buggers off of him. The couch fell backwards, dumping him into the field. He stood up and ran into the clearing.

The rest of the group made their way haphazardly to the path that led them around the curve of the field. The path was narrow, and they had to run single-file.

"They are…so…fast," Belmont panted. One was snapping wildly at his ears every once in a while grabbing some hair and plucking it from his head.

The birds continued jumping up and snapping at the group. Every time one would land a bite it would hang on ferociously.

Rachel successfully dodged one toothy-chick, but it landed on Gilly's shoulder and promptly bit her ear.

"WOW. Ooch! Ooh, that was not nice," she said, rubbing her ear forcefully. "I hate you. I hate you so much!"

A few more of the goozlings were running among their feet nipping at their ankles and toes. Rachel had one attached to her boot. It chomped upwards and finally bit flesh at her calf.

"Mother!!" Rachel yelped.

Another one flew towards Rachel's face and she stopped it with her hand. She stuck out her tongue and the sharp little beak snapped at it. Just barely, but not quite, missing the tip.

"Muffa!" she said, and grabbed her mouth. The bird in her hand then crashed into her face, but luckily bounced off and was left behind.

The path curved and they found themselves near the crates where he and Dante originally hid. The adult Goozels were still lolling in the sun and absentmindedly grazing on onion roots.

Harry was making more army-man gestures, which no one was watching. He was cutting across the field running towards the fat lazy adults.

Once again, Belmont jumped over the crates and charged the flock of dumb birds in the middle of the field. This time the screaming and arm flapping was not pretend.

As they approached, the chicks seemed to get even more terrifying. They would screech as they leaped in the air, flap furiously to get a little altitude and plunge their pin-sized daggers in the skin of their victims.

The two groups of kids were reaching the grazing birds at exactly the same time from opposite ends.

"Watch where you're going." Harry yelled. "Look out!" Monty yelled.

"Turn left," they both yelled, and promptly collided – hard. Fortunately, a fat Goozel got caught in the middle and broke their impact.

An explosion of feathers clouded the area for a moment and there was complete chaos. The two flocks of pursuing chicks overshot their targets and were confused as soon as they hit the group of adults. They drifted around the fallen kids like puffs of snow.

Harry and Belmont untangled themselves and ran again for the edge of the clearing. The other two groups joined them and ran past the couch and up the original path.

They stopped a few yards up panting heavily. A few fell down on their knees. All of them were exhausted and out of breath. They looked around taking stock of each other. Around the group, no one had escaped the onslaught of chicks. There were bleeding ears and noses. Their hands, necks and faces were poked a dozen places with tiny little blood marks. There were bald patches of hair and Rachel had a black eye. They all had white and yellow feathers floating around their ears and tangled in their hair.

"Well, that was successful," said Rachel sarcastically.

"Ohh, I hate those little birds!" said Gilly, holding a tuft of her orange hair in her hands.

Belmont said, "I wouldn't call it a complete failure, I guess," and they all looked at him. He held up a fat adult Goozel by the leg.

"I kinda ran into this one, and I guess I forgot to let go."

They all looked stunned. Harry was the first to recover and laughed. "You know, I guess you aren't so worthless after all," he clapped him on the back. "Tonight, we feast!"

———

That night around the fire, the kids were telling stories about the day's adventures and their mishaps with the Goozels. They were sharing delicious bites of tender baked bird that Dante had prepared over the campfire.

"You should have seen her, Apple," Harry was laughing, "... one minute Gilly's yelling at us not to hurt the little buggers... and two minutes later, she's telling us to squash them."

"I didn't say *squash* them," she protested, "I just said...'I hate them'," she said embarrassedly.

Apple was sad to have missed the excitement. But she got over it quickly with a pile of roast Goozel on her plate. Magnus didn't seem bothered either way. He was just gnawing on a giant sized drumstick (which looked about the right size for his huge hand).

Dante had prepared the bird perfectly. He even suggested that it didn't need much seasoning, as they mostly fed on onions and herbs anyway.

"He says the flavors are already baked right into them," said Martin, interpreting for Dante. Then he whispered, "like we didn't hear him the first six times!" But he smiled at his brother as he reached for a third helping.

They were having a great time. Everyone was poking fun at each other and their reaction to being attacked by such little predators. Martin had recalled that the birds had a sort of backwards evolution. Instead of growing up to be more aggressive and better fighters as they got older, the birds are actually born aggressive and became more docile as they got bigger.

"It makes a lot of sense down here," explained Martin. "I mean think about it, there's not a ton of predators. Mostly, the only time the birds are threatened is when they're little. And if they're very aggressive…"

Gilly chimed in rubbing her ear, "Oh, they're very aggressive!"

"Yeah, if they're very aggressive, they can protect themselves."

"Even from Martin's deadly bow," chided Rachel.

Harry threw the wishbone at her, "I didn't see you bringing home any trophies!"

The laughter and talking continued late into the night. Even though they were all sore and had makeshift bandages on dozens of sores, they all were proud of their victory. Apple leaned over from her perch and handed Belmont something. She palmed it into his hand and he opened it. It was one of those plastic spider rings – orange and missing a leg.

"Present for hunter Belmonty," Belmont put it on and went to hug Apple as thanks. She frowned and skittered away up the garbage mound a bit. But she looked pleased with herself anyway.

"Ooh. Someone's got a crush on you." Harry whistled.

Apple promptly threw a gnawed Goozel bone his way and stuck out her tongue.

"Don't tease her." Rachel snapped at Harry. And then to Monty, "It does mean something though. It means you're part of the tribe."

"Tribe, huh?" Monty rubbed the waxy orange spider ring and noted the one leg had been seemingly chewed off by its prior owner.

"Yeah. We all have one." Rachel held up her hand to show a similar plastic ring "crawling" up her finger.

Behind her, Harry thumped his chest before holding his spider clad hand in the air. Dante followed, then Martin. Gilly squeaked when she put hers in the air and big Marcus held a fist straight out showing a pink plastic ring choking his thick pinky knuckle. Finally Apple pointed an aggressive finger Monty's way before smiling shyly, and then held up a blue spidered finger.

Belmont was happy. He was part of something here. They had all seemingly forgotten about his very small role in creating this prison that they all were stuck in. In fact, it didn't feel so much like a prison anymore. It started to feel a little bit more like…home.

Beach

The sun had crested, the air was warm and they had leftover Goozel meat for breakfast. They were walking down towards the lake. All was good.

The water shimmered in front of them like a bowl of glass shards. They came to a small beachhead that ended in a tall piece of machinery at the end. A large cable extended from the top of the winch across the water to the far side.

"It's actually kinda beautiful." commented Monty wistfully. But then he regained the reality of The Can, "But are you sure it's safe? I don't want to come out of there with blue spots or scales and fins."

Rachel flashed him a look.

"Oh it's safe. We've been swimming here loads of times, and look at how normal we are." Martin held his arms forward presenting himself.

It was not lost on him that he wore a stained canary-yellow shirt that read "Beach Bums" over a picture of a hobo sleeping on the sand.

"Oh, great. Thanks, I'll pass," Belmont laughed.

"You and me both." Rachel commented.

"What, you're not going swimming?" Monty asked her.

"Nope and never."

"Don't bother about her, she's afraid of the water," said Harry.

"It's not that I'm afraid of the water, I just think it's kind of disgusting."

"What do you mean? You shower in it." Harry retorted.

"Well that's different. That's not saltwater. And I'm using soap."

"Well then here you go," Harry said and flipped her a bottle cap size nub of Irish Spring.

"Ha ha you're so funny," and she chucked it back at him.

"Well, you drink this water, you know."

Rachel looked at Belmont for support, and was stung when he responded with, "I'm sorry. I'm oddly with Harry on this one. Saltwater isn't harmful. If you could swim, come join us."

"You're afraid of the water, aren't you? Scaredy-cat!" Harrison jumped in and started splashing around then he splashed at Rachel.

"DON'T YOU DARE! Do not splash me!" The venom in her voice stopped the group cold.

Awkward silence hung heavy while Rachel stomped around collecting a few things on the beach and then looked back at them..

"I am going back. Apple, do you want to come?"

"Can I tell you something? I really like fishies and I really like swimming and I really like water and I also like swimmies... and, can I tell you something, else..."

"Fine! If you're gonna stay, I'll see you back at the fort." She whipped her hair around and stomped back up the path.

"Sheesh – what's her problem?" Harrison said.

"I don't know. That was a little more emotional than the situation warranted," Monty said, curiously looking at her as she disappeared up the path.

"Never mind. Girls are weird. Even JYK girls," Harrison had undressed down to a pair of tight fitting yellow shorts. They had a grinning panda on the backside.

Apple pointed and laughed, "Girls are weird? Boys are weirdos. Look at you."

Harrison didn't pay attention. Instead he scrambled up the ladder of the winching equipment. It was sort of like a ski lift suspended from the lighting grid above.

Harry balanced out to a bar that was hanging a few feet out from shore. He swung down to sit on the hanging bar and proceeded to lower himself to the water. He took a skateboard deck – without wheels, that hung from a hook on the supporting beam, and floated it underneath him.

He gave a thumbs-up to Dante, who had positioned himself inside the lift mechanics. A winch sounded, gears clanged together and all of a sudden the bar that Harrison was holding was jerked forward towards the deep end of the lake. The board slanted underneath Harry, he leaned far back and used the T-bar to steady himself. Then he took off across the water.

"Whoo-Hoo," Harrison jettisoned across the smooth surface of the lake, and was able to carve back and forth underneath the wire-pulley system that hung across the water. He skimmed along that way for about a quarter-mile towards the other side of the lake. He was quickly approaching where the cables turned around another large winch.

Harrison zipped close to the other shore as he wound around the pole to the other side of the pulley system. Then he was returning with nice speed. He got back to their side of the beach and let go of the bar to come sliding on the water right up the beach to end up standing on the sand in front of Monty.

"Ha. That was great wasn't it. Whew! This is the best thing we get to do down here. If I ever escaped, I think I may actually miss this." And then Harry said to Belmont, "You want to try?"

Monty had water-skied before at summer camp. He wasn't amazing, exactly, but he was good enough to impress this group. He was feeling brave, so he grabbed the board from the shallows, and reached for the hanging bar.

"Okay. Get your feet like this. That's right, and kind of lean back like that. Yep. That's good." Harrison was being as friendly to Monty as he could remember.

"Feeling secure? Good. Now remember, that's HazMat Beach over there. Just hang back in the shallows as the line pulls around the winch. Don't stop over there. Got it. Excellent."

"And when you're ready, give Dante a thumbs up like this," and he raised his thumb high.

Dante mistakenly thought it was the signal and jammed the winch into motion. The bar jolted forward, half yanking Monty's arm out of his socket. He wobbled forward, tottered with his footing, and almost fell before getting out of the knee deep shallows.

But he recovered nicely. He kept his feet on the board, and the board was relatively steady. As Belmont got farther into the lake, he started to gain his confidence. He tried to shift his weight and carve to one side, with the thick cable above him, and then to the other side of the cable. He passed another pole in the center of the lake, and splashed some wake at it.

"Whoo!" he was having fun now. He reached down and dragged a finger in the calm surface of the water, and it made a cutting noise. A small fish leapt at his finger, thinking it was a meal, and bounded over Belmont's hand. In that short burst from the water, Monty noticed the fish had two little tails, as it disappeared with a flash of gold under the surface.

He was approaching the far end of the lake, and saw the turning wheel ahead. He decided to cut as close as he could to shore, to show off a bit (even though he was probably a bit too far from the rest of the group to notice). He cut in towards shore and was leaning hard when his board caught something small just under the surface of the water and was ripped out from underneath him.

He flipped headlong and splashed hard in the water. His momentum was strong so that it somersaulted him twice before he stood up in the shallow water. He gasped for air and then sneezed and coughed the water out of his nose. It took him a moment to get his breath, before he lost it again.

He had just wiped out…worse yet, he had just wiped out on HazMat Beach.

HazMat

Dante must have seen Monty go down, because the bar stopped a few yards out over the water. Monty looked across the lake and could just make out Dante waving an orange cloth over his head as he leaned out of the winch operator chair.

Monty waved back, and rubbed the water from his eyes. He looked around for the board and saw it on the edge of shore, bobbing on the small waves left from his wake.

The beach was short, and ended in a wall of trash higher than his head. It looked nastier, and smelled much worse, than their side of The Can. There seemed to be a few breaks in the wall of garbage which opened to dark passages into the HazMat zone.

It gave Belmont the creeps and he shivered involuntarily. The few hints he had heard about this side of The Can was enough to keep Belmont on his toes. He wanted to get out of here as soon as he could. He nervously made his way over to the board trying to step quietly.

As he lifted the board up, and turned to swim out to the T-bar, he noticed something small moving in the sand on the edge of the trash wall. It was dark brown and fuzzy and it was seemingly twisting on itself like a snake.

Monty curiously stepped out of the water towards the movement. Closer up it looked more like two small snakes. Or a few snakes. But they were fuzzy – actually *furry*. He leaned in to study the animal more clearly.

It would be best to describe it as a brown, furry octopus about the size of a football. It was impossible for Belmont to count the legs as it writhed, but it may have had only five or six, and it seemed almost cuddly. It was twisting its legs around something and its shiny fur rippled as it moved.

Belmont saw something silver and metallic underneath the Furzopus and recognized it as a double-D battery. The animal seemed to be squeezing it. Or rubbing it. Or something else. Was it *sucking* on it?

It was. The little beast seemed to be using its legs to wind the battery towards a little rubbery mouth that was making suckling noises on the battery. Monty squatted back to watch this weird looking creature nurse its "battery-bottle".

"It's feeding." He thought to himself. "What an odd..."

But his thoughts were interrupted by a loud WHOMP! As a hairy claw punched through a black garbage bag immediately behind the little creature. The claw grabbed the Furrpus hard, making it squeak like a dog toy. Its tentacles squirmed through its grip and then hung limp around the massive paw.

The claw continued to grip the furry creature, tearing through the garbage bag as the paw was raised higher to the top of the trash wall. And there, just above Belmont, was the fiercest looking monster Belmont could have imagined.

Belmont froze, absolutely terrified. He knew immediately it was one of those beasts they had seen on BioSide. But from this close up, it was worse than he could have imagined.

A huge head, the size of a watermelon, was sitting neckless on massive shoulders. Two huge ape-like arms hung over the refuse wall with bits of torn trash-bag hanging from the hairy, muscled forearms. Two yellow fangs protruded upwards from a heavy jaw, and drool oozed from its curled-back lips.

But the eyes were what made Belmont shiver with fear.

The eyes Protruded from the sunken brow like two short stubs of an elephant trunk – with similar gray wrinkled skin to match. The meaty tubes extended for a few inches from the face and ended in bulbous yellow eyeballs framed by heavy grey lids. The entire "snout" of one eye was swiveled to look at the furry creature it held, while the other eye scanned the horizon with its dark pupil.

The monster stuffed the Furzopus into its mouth, which gave a sad little squeak. The beast spit out the battery with a soft pop, and caught the object in its claw. Its eyes swiveled to get a closer look at the object in its paw, as it chewed and swallowed what was left of the furry creature.

The Morge was so large it stood a head and shoulders over the wall of trash. But it was facing the lake so it didn't notice Belmont at the foot of the wall. If it were to turn and look down, it would surely see him shivering in its shadow. He crouched closer to the bottom of the wall.

The beast brought the battery up to its nose, sniffed and tested the object with its lips. Then it palmed it in its huge paw, like a human might hide a mint, and loped backwards into the darkness of the garbage behind it.

Belmont was afraid to move for another ten minutes or so. And even then, he crept back to the lake, and slinked as quietly as he could to the t-bar out over the water. He desperately hoped that Dante could see him as he raised his thumb as high, and as quietly, as he could.

After a brief pause, Belmont heard the winch kick in, and a strong tug yanked him out of the water. Even though he knew it was pointless at this point, he tried to crouch down to stay hidden from those terrible eyes. For a few horrible seconds, he was sure the beast would come charging out of the waste and grab for him in the shallow water. But, as he approached the center pole, he ventured a glance backwards.

The beach looked empty. There was no sign of the monster that had cast a shadow over Belmont a few terrifying moments before. He wiped his brow of water spray and sweat, and focused on getting to the safe side of the lake.

This World Has Changed

That night, as they roasted apples and peaches around Magma, Belmont told the group what he had seen on HazMat. After telling the story, the group sat stunned.

Dante was the first to comment. *"Lo vi caer, pero no pude verlo al otro lado del lago."*

"Yeah, until he came back shaking like a leaf." Martin said, "...and rightfully so," he added quickly.

"The Morge was terrifying. I thought I was a goner. But, I wonder what it was doing with the battery? And for that matter, the Furzopus. Do these things eat batteries?"

"I've seen one of those before. It wasn't on a battery or anything. It was wriggling around on the winch line a few weeks ago." Harry said.

"I've never seen one before," responded Monty. "But I guess there are a lot of animals here that I haven't seen before. I know the firm was trying to round up any, uh, unnaturals."

"What is 'the firm'?" Gilly asked curiously.

"The company that built this place... And is supposed to be managing it. Global Waste and Hazardous Material Processing Company, or GWAHMP Co. But I hadn't realized they had relocated so many...*animals*."

"We call them NewBeasts." Harry started. He could tell he had an audience, so he continued in a more theatrical tone.

"Nature has a way of adapting, and she has had to work overtime to keep up with the pollution. New breeds of plants and animals – and some rather unpleasant breeds, I might add – developed in the most polluted regions."

"That's right. We've all heard the stories," Harry continued. "Giant slugs, some ten feet long, in city sewers. Gnarled vines of unidentified flora wound in septic tanks, belching soot into the air from black flowers. Long-tongued fish, with bulging eyes and green scales, caught slinking into schools through the drain pipes and toilets… it seems the stories were true."

"I remember seeing a featherless bird with a twisted beak burrowing in a soup can." Gilly pitched in. "I thought it was cute," she ended shyly.

"But it wasn't just the smaller creatures of the world that were affected." Harry was on a roll with his story and he continued talking as though he was telling a ghost story around a campfire. "Yellow-toothed Doglings and squelchy hairless Catses would howl at each other from the peaks of fermented apple cores, coffee grounds and greasy engine parts. Reptiles of immense size and bulk were found in warmer climates, wedged into drainage gullies; unmoving and swallowing everything that would find its way down into its jagged oily maw."

"Belmonty. Guess what. I think you met one of those. You know Giganticgator right?" Added Apple. "He's funny!"

"Meanwhile, the garbage continued to gather, the muck continued to mount, the sewage continued to swell and the trash continued to amass. And through it all, suspicious and mysterious new plants and animals developed – and the rest of the world watched nervously."

Rachel groaned at his theatrics. "Get on with it Harry, we don't have all night. Some of us would like to go to sleep *eventually*."

"Every living thing that came into contact with the vast amounts of waste was changing. Rats and 'coons, snakes and lizards, everything that swam, slank or slithered, crawled, flew or burrowed, or even walked – on four legs…or on *two*." Harry paused for dramatic effect. "That's right, even the most *intelligent* of creatures were undergoing some drastic, and not so pleasant, changes."

"Can I tell you something, I don't think I like this story." Apple peeped, and burrowed her head further into her blanket.

"Some of our less fortunate fellow human beings were transformed – or evolved – into these ape-like creatures. Morges are the most terrible creatures in the world. They are frighteningly awful beasts. Dreadfully nauseating. They are a revoltingly horrendous, disgustingly repugnant, hideously disfigured, regurgitated breed of man."

"They are filthy, stinky, stanky animals…" Apple's voice was a bit muffled from under the blanket.

"Well, *Manimals*, anyway," added Martin.

"And their hair is so gross." Finished Gilly.

"*Se asemejan a Magnus, si decidió vestirse con un abrigo de piel vieja,*" chuckled Dante. Magnus, hearing his name, shifted his huge bulk uncomfortably close to Dante, who immediately stopped smiling.

"Their hair grows in tangled disheveled clumps. They come in colors of brown, black, red, blonde, grey – and even some bluish, greenish, or magenta varieties. Remember, this is all on one Morge!"

Even Rachel laughed at that.

"But the hairy parts of these beasts are not the most terrifying. And neither are their upward turned sweaty fangs. Or even their stubby tails or knobbed flappy feet. Surprisingly, neither are their elongated arms, spiked elbow joints, or their excruciatingly painful breath, although that's probably close…"

"It's their eyes." Belmont's tone brought the mood back down, and everyone turned to look at him. He sat for a moment staring into the orange and red swirls of Magma, before he continued, "Absolutely terrifying."

Pier

The sun was shining immediately centered in the mouth of the canyon a few miles or so above his head. Belmont was peddling a strange contraption of a bike that Martin had cobbled together out of spare parts found in The Can. He was looking for Rachel and thought he spotted her silhouette on a pier by Reservoir.

Rachel was standing at the end of the pier, looking at the open water spread out in front of her. The sparkling lake outlined her silhouette. Belmont was again stricken with an unknown emotion. Something that made him simultaneously want to go to her and leave at the same time.

As he laid the rusty bike down and stepped on the pier, the sun flashed on the lake and cast an odd shadow on Rachel. It gave a strange halo of something on her bare legs, like spines or some prickly cloth. He paused for a few moments as she turned around to the sound of his footsteps on the wooden pier.

"Oh, hey. Belmont, give me a minute," she said, scrambling with a towel.

Belmont looked away embarrassed for a moment, thinking she didn't have "appropriate" clothes on. Then he remembered her dislike of swimming.

She toweled off, and kept holding up her finger in a "just one more minute" signal. Then she wrapped the towel around her hair, collected a few things on the dock and slowly walked towards Belmont.

"I thought you didn't like the water?" Belmont said.

"Oh. Yeah, I don't. I won't swim in that lake."

"But, why are you drying off?"

"I got splashed when I was watching the other shore for…oh, hey is that a new bike?" Rachel quickly changed the subject as she pointed to the pink jalopy leaning against the post.

"Dante had been working on it. He thought it allowed us to get from Point A to Point B faster."

"I bet it does. It also gets you from Point A to Point *Dork* faster, too. Not that you needed help." She hoisted herself onto the banana seat, rang the little princess bell and blew a kiss to Belmont. Then she peddled up the path towards the fort, leaving Belmont weirdly annoyed, amused and satisfied at the same time.

Mushrooms

That evening, after they had all gone to bed, Belmont was woken by his mattress swaying wildly. It was still dark and his eyes needed to adjust. When they finally did, he saw Dante standing over him rocking his weight back and forth. He was grinning impishly.

"Dante? What are you doing? It's late..."

"*No. Es temprano. Has dormido lo suficiente. Es hora de ir. Hora de cosechar.*" He responded.

"I don't understand you, but understand this: I. Am. Sleeping." And Belmont rolled over and hugged his blanket over his head.

Dante stood for a moment with his hands on his hips. Then he grabbed the rope that Monty used to swing into bed each night and pushed his weight onto one foot. The stack of mattresses leaned dangerously far, and Belmont rolled towards the side.

At the last moment he grabbed the corner of the mattress as his feet slid off the edge. His blanket and pillow fell ten feet to the floor.

"All right, all right. I'm awake." Belmont yawned. He was gingerly scaling down his mattress tower. "But *why* am I awake, is the question?"

Dante performed an athletic hop halfway down the tower to a mattress corner jutting out, and then again to the bottom. He beat Belmont by a full two seconds. "Okay. So, what's up?" Monty asked, annoyed that Dante had beat him to the bottom.

Dante smiled, *"Vamos a cosechar,"* he paused, and then said in plain English, "Mushrooms!"

Belmont was still rubbing the sleep out of his eyes as they walked down a dark path. Dante was chattering to Belmont still in Spanish as he led them in a new direction from the fort.

The lighting grid had not yet gone on for the morning, and it was extremely dark. Belmont struggled to see more than a few feet ahead of him. Fortunately, Dante had tied a child's glow stick around his arm. It made following him easier, at least.

Dante came to a stop and listened. He motioned for Belmont to put his backpack down, and then he crawled forward under a tangled mess of wires and other garbage. They crept slowly forward on their hands and knees with Belmont following. They soon came to an impenetrable mound of trash. At the bottom, there was a large plastic bin laying sideways, with a hole gnawed through the bottom. The opening led to a dark crevasse behind it.

"Esta es la apertura a una colonia de hormigas," Dante said.

"Hey. You've been down here long enough. Why can't you speak English like everyone else... Well except for maybe Magnus?"

"Shhh!" Dante clocked him on top of his head, a finger to his lips, "BigAnts. Mushrooms." He pointed in the hole.

It took Belmont a second to register, "Oh! BigAnts, yeah. They cultivate mushrooms, don't they." He said, finally understanding what they were doing.

"Todavía está oscuro. Las hormigas no estarán en casa. Vamos a cenar." Dante flashed that impish smile again and entered the hole. Belmont looked around and reluctantly followed.

They were plunged into complete and total darkness. The dark was so present, that you could feel it like a weight. Randomly, Belmont could see the glow-stick bracelet on Dante's arm, as he crawled in front with a purpose.

They seemed to take a dozen left turns, and Belmont wondered how they hadn't gone in a circle. But then he realized the tunnel was on a slight decline, so they were descending slowly, like taking a long and very dark spiral staircase.

A hazy blue glow started to illuminate the tunnel. As they rounded a bend, they came into a larger cavern where dozens of tiny blue mushrooms glowed faintly on every surface.

Dante turned towards Belmont with a proud look on his face. Belmont shared his enthusiasm, and they both whispered "Mushrooms!" to each other.

Gathering the mushrooms was easy work. They didn't need to enter far to have a few dozen of the smallish bluish glowish fungi. They each had collected more than they could comfortably carry in less than half hour. They ascended the tunnel and emerged from the hole. Dante started to sort the fungi into easier to carry bunches, but a noise stopped them mid-motion.

It was a gruff animal sound, somewhat between a snort and a snuff. They stared at each other in the dark, not moving. Then they heard rustling just outside of the clearing.

"My backpack," Belmont mouthed silently to Dante pointing towards the trail. He had left it just outside so he could fit in the hole.

Dante furrowed his brow confused, then nodded understanding. They both crawled a few feet towards the opening that led to the path and leaned forward.

It was pitch black, but they could sense someone, or something, on the path ahead of them. It was huge, and it hunkered over something on the ground. Belmont thought he heard the sound of a bare foot on a loose slab of tile, and then he saw a silhouetted hump of huge shoulders standing in the path.

"Magnus!" He almost called out, but something made him hold his tongue. And then the smell hit him like a slap to the face. It stung his eyes and his throat, like fresh vomit. He stifled a gag, but made a slight choking noise. The shoulders straightened and a huge hairy head came up into view over the massive back. It slowly started to turn towards them and they could hear it sniffing the air loudly.

Dante grabbed Monty's arm and started to pull him back when suddenly, the lighting grid kicked on. Although the light was muted, it illuminated the dark path immediately. They could see the beast that was holding Monty's backpack with one long arm dragging on the ground. In the other, it held something small and black in front of its face.

The light caused the beast to flinch, and it looked up at the light source. It paused for a moment then held the black square to its nose sniffing loudly one last time before dropping it, and the bag, back on the path. The beast then slowly loped away from the fort, passing the two kids cowering in the hole.

We Need to Escape

"**W**e have to get out of here. We will not survive with those things down here with us..." Monty pleaded.

"*Especialmente porque vienen a la puerta de nuestra casa.*" Dante argued.

They had just briefed the group on their most recent Morge sighting. The group was stunned at how close the monster was to their front door.

"Sure, of course. But, what are we supposed to do, call the police?" Harry said sarcastically.

"Well, I have a cell phone..."

All of the JYKs' eyebrows went up and jaws went slack.

"... But no battery."

Everyone's eyes went back down dejectedly with a sigh of disappointment.

"It fell out when I was being chased by the evil doctor." Belmont continued. "Interestingly, that's what the Morge was smelling when we saw it this morning."

"*Es una pena que tengas un teléfono tan antiguo. Tenemos muchos cables de carga.*" Dante held up a long rope he had made by braiding all sorts of discarded cords together.

"But that won't help us without a battery. Who has detachable batteries, anymore?" Harrison finished.

"People throw away batteries all the time," said Martin.

"Yeah," Gilly responded, "Even though they are not supposed to throw them away. They're really bad for the environment, you know."

"It doesn't matter. They'd go to HazMat anyway. Batteries, especially cell phone batteries, are toxic." Rachel said.

"You know, batty-ries are bad. They can hurt mountain gorillas, lowland gorillas, western gorillas – maybe other animals too." Apple chimed in.

"We could try to go get some…" Harry said.

The group went silent thinking about the danger involved going to HazMat. Rachel was the one to break the silence.

"No good, anyway. They'd all be dead. The batteries, that is… and probably us too, if we went over there. They'd have no charge. We got a phone and charge cords, sure. But they do us no good if they're all dead – because we have no electricity."

"We do have some electricity. The lighting grid works." Martin pointed upwards.

Everyone looked up at the large mesh gridwork way above their heads. The evening lights were starting to come on, warming up with a steady humming noise.

"What would that do?" Asked Harry, "We can't reach that high. Even Peke isn't close to the lights."

"Maybe not, but Morge Mountain might be… and that's where we'd find the batteries anyway."

Silence again.

"What? Are you crazy?! You mean to say we should go wander over to HazMat. Collect a bunch of dead batteries. Hike up Morge Mountain. Scale to the lighting grid. Plug-in, charge up, call out – and order pizza!?"

"I didn't say order pizza," Belmont muttered.

But some of the JYKs were lost in thought. Harry was slowly nodding and Gilly was chewing on a lock of hair.

"I know it's dangerous, but I think it could work." Monty said thinking out loud. "And I think I have a plan."

NewBeasts

"So are these…*monsters*…the former workers of this facility? Did they *change* into these things?" Belmont asked.

"No, I don't think so. Well, I guess we don't know for sure. They have been here as long as we have, probably longer. But we've never actually seen any workers here before." Rachel responded.

"Yeah, no other humans…well, adults anyway." Gilly added, looking around at her comrades.

Martin looked up from his soup, "No, they're not the workers. These Morges did evolve from humans, but many years ago. The story has it that some refugees that had been taking cover in some vacated sewers underneath New York or Chicago or something like that, slowly started to evolve into these beasts."

"Yeah. I remember hearing about that. I thought they flooded them out or something?" Harrison interrupted.

"That's right. They did. I guess they survived and ended up here…. So while they did evolve from humans, they came from someplace else. Not the old GWAHMP workers."

Belmont recounted his story of hearing his dad on the phone, and his worry about the workers *changing*. He also mentioned his conversation with his friend Louis who was concerned because he lost contact with his mom.

"See, that's what I don't understand. My dad had gotten so worked up about the workers *changing*. He specifically used that word. He was trying to shut this facility down because of it. But he never got to do so. So where did the workers go, if these Morges aren't them?"

"Well, whatever they are, I wish they would go back to the hole they crawled out from. That goes for most of these creatures." Harrison grumbled, poking at a wandering BigAnt that was getting too close to the group.

"C'mon. All of the NewBeasts aren't bad or terrible. Some are cute. Have you ever seen Red-Berry Birds? O. M. Gee! They are adorable. They're cherry red, about as big as ladybugs and their little beaks sort of curl up into this delicious little smile." Gilly giggled.

They were eating a feast of the mushrooms Belmont and Dante had collected from the BigAnts that morning. The JYKs were trying to stay in a positive mood since coming up with such a ridiculously dangerous mission, so the shift in conversation from Morges was welcome.

"Or Wumpins! Ooo, I just want to eatem' up." Gilly said, squeezing her guitar until it hummed with energy.

"You know. I like BunnyBunBuns." Apple said, waggling her stuffed animal.

"Well, BunnyBunBuns isn't exactly *real*…" Belmont said, but before he could finish his sentence, Apple clunked him in the head with a peach pit.

"I suppose Fuzzels are kinda cute," said Rachel begrudgingly.

"O.M. Geez! Fuzzels and Fozzels are both so cute!!" Gilly hugged harder and her guitar hummed again.

"Really? Fozzels??" questioned Martin. "Aren't they kind of, I dunno, gravely? I'd much prefer Porcupoos. Those are cool."

"I love NagraHorns, even though they only eat clothes.… Ya know, my friend Miles said he saw two of them playing tug of war with an old bra!"

Everyone laughed at that.

"I've always been partial to these BigAnts." Belmont said. A few JYKs nodded in agreement.

"*Y las setas están _deliciosas!_*" said Dante, raising a plump mushroom cap as a toast to their dinner. Belmont smiled, not understanding a word, but recognizing the reference to the meal he helped produce.

"You know what are the coolest?" said Harry from the shadows of Magma. Everyone quieted down and looked back at him. "Viper Violets," he hissed.

Magnus backed up a bit, and Gilly loosened her huggy-grip. Apple popped her hoodie over her face and Dante chuckled nervously.

"*Eso no es real.*"

"Yes they are. They grow without sunlight, and their flowers are inky black, like a wet midnight. They're said to be able to burrow into your dreams if you let them. They silently slide in on you if you're not careful, and blow a puff of Viper pollen into your face."

"What?? C'mon," protested Rachel.

"I've heard that too. And the pollen paralyzes you. You freeze." Martin said, agreeing.

"No. It doesn't paralyze you. That would be too kind. It turns you into a...Zombie!" he startled the group and they all jumped back. Apple squeaked and Magnus put his ham-sized hands in front of his face.

"And then you go looking for other unsuspecting people to cough pollen into their faces, until everyone you know is undead!"

Everyone sat quietly contemplating this situation, until Belmont broke the silence.

"Well I don't know anything about Silent but Violent Vipers or whatever."

"Viper Violets," grumped Harry, annoyed that the spooky energy didn't last longer.

"But I do know about the most wonderful NewBeast on the planet."

"Miliwebbers are! You know what, they have spider-webbys built into their legs. They are so fun, you can make a net out of them." Apple chirped.

"No, you are missing the best one," Belmont said mysteriously.

Gilly jumped in "How about Munyons? Did you know they are the only bird that can swim, fly and burrow..."

"Nope. It's...Mermaids!"

Mermaids

"Ooo, Mermaids. Those are legendary." Martin responded. "Not often seen, but wonderful nonetheless. Do you know the story of the lost mermaid mothers?" Martin looked around at the faces around the fire slowly shaking their heads, no.

"They say that in Japan, a whole bunch of babies were born with tails instead of legs…"

"I thought it was Ireland." Harry interrupted, clearly jealous that this story was more interesting than his Viper Violets.

"Same thing. They're both islands. Anyway, the babies could breathe underwater and swim as fast as dolphins. Their DNA was trying to adapt to the polluted world by being able to live underwater."

"Right, like the oceans weren't polluted?" Rachel snapped, disbelieving.

"Not as bad, anyway. And not really down down deep. There it's not as polluted. But the babies could live on land as well. Something like their tails turned into legs or something."

"But the governments were concerned. Were they a threat to normal humans? Or could they be used as weapons? There was a crackdown on Mermaids and they were rounded up."

"Obviously, the families tried to hide the children. And the easiest place to hide a mermaid is in the ocean. So, they let them all go. Dozens of mothers brought their children to remote locations in the middle of the ocean – and let them go. And that's where they live to this day."

"And once every year, when the moon is full and silvery, all of the mermaids go back to Japan…or Ireland…and sing to the moon about their lost mothers."

"Oh no. That's so saddy-sad. I want the little mermaid babies to have their mommy-moms." Apple cried.

"Now we're getting fantastical. Mermaids don't exist, no more than Harry's Silent but Violent farting flowers." Rachel barked.

"They do too. And they're beautiful with silver hair and covered with green scales…"

"No they don't…" she snapped back.

"…and they have big, beautiful…"

"Mermaids DO NOT EXIST!" Rachel screamed, and Martin stopped short. Everyone paused sensing her worst temper.

And then, quietly Belmont interjected. "That's not true. They do exist. And I've seen one."

Everyone turned to look at Belmont.

"It's true. When I was about two or three years old, on the day that my dad conjured up this facility in his mind, a mermaid came to me in my sandpit."

Apple squeaked.

"I don't know if they are *all* beautiful, but this one was. And her hair shimmered, but from the sun and not because it was silver. She rose up from the waves just as the tide came in. She smiled down at me and said, 'Hello there little one, how did you get trapped down there.' Then she reached in, picked me up and set me next to my father. She kissed me on my forehead and dove back into the water, and never came back up. One thing is incorrect about your story. She didn't have a tail. Instead she had *two*. They looked more like legs, but with fins…"

"That's it. I've had enough!" Rachel interrupted. "First Harry's farting flowers and now we're talking about two tailed girls that live in the ocean and kiss babies? This is ridiculous and I'm done with this conversation." She stood up to go. "And thanks again for bringing up the fact that you and your absentee father invented this catastrophe we live in. I was just starting to forget that inconvenient fact."

She threw the rest of her meal onto Magma, where it quickly puffed into a ball of smoke.

"And don't count me in with this ridiculous escape plan either. Any dope stupid enough to believe in fairy tales, is not worth following to our death!"

And with that, she stormed off across Glen and out of one of the many exits.

Makeup

Rachel was sitting on a stack of palettes in a small clearing looking up at the silver moon. The moon was centered overhead with the rim of The Canyon circling it with a dark halo. Rachel was quietly making sounds. Talking? Crying? ...No, it was singing. Very faintly she was singing with just a few words breaking above a whisper like they were surfacing for air.

He recognized that it was some sort of lullaby, and it made Monty's eyes sting. He quietly squatted down behind an old couch and listened intently. He felt a little guilty for spying on this tender moment, but curiosity got the better of him. Curiosity and...sadness. Or was it something else? Yes. It was deeper than just sadness. It was a feeling of deep loneliness. The song was beautiful but it made him feel like the only person left in the world.

The full moon stared at them through the backward end of the miles-long telescope. He felt like the smallest creature on the planet; utterly lost and absolutely alone. He sat there scared and sad and lonely and rubbed at his eyes.

His palm came away damp and he noticed a small tear drop clinging to the orange spider ring Apple had given him earlier that week.

He stared at it for a few moments, absently rubbing the tear droplet into the waxy rubber ring. The ring reminded him of Apple. And it reminded him of Rachel. Which reminded him of the others. And it reminded him of all the things they'd done to help him, and all the things he'd learned down here. And he remembered he wasn't alone.

He straightened himself up, gave his face a final rub, and stood up. He took a deep breath and walked towards Rachel.

He didn't want to startle her so he shuffled his feet a bit and cleared his throat. He didn't want to scare her, but he also thought she might've been crying.

"Rachel, are you alright?"

"What…. Ya… Yes. I am… I'm just…" She hastily rubbed her eyes, and turned away from him embarrassed.

"Rachel, listen. We are thousands of miles from civilization and miles underwater. We are lost in a cavern populated with monsters. We've lost our homes. We've lost our families. And we are all scared. But what we are *not* is alone."

"We are not *alone*. There are eight people down here who need each other. We are a band of lost souls, but we are lost – *together*. The only way we can make this work is by being together."

Rachel snorted, but only half-heartedly.

"Rachel, Apple needs you. So do Dante and Martin. And so does Marcus. Even that Butthead Harrison needs you." Rachel stifled a laugh at that. "And Rachel, *I* need you. And you need us. Let's not split up. It's silly. It's dumb actually, and dangerous. Let's figure out a way to make this work. Together."

"Well, do you think this battery idea might work?" Rachel sniffed.

"It will work! But only with your help. So are we gonna do this?"

Rachel looked up at the moon for a moment and finally said, "The moon reminds me of my mother. You know, it doesn't really look that much farther away here than what I remember from home."

"It wouldn't. The moon is about 240,000 miles away. Adding a few miles would hardly…" he responded logically, but stopped and noticed Rachel looking back down at the ground. He started again, differently this time.

"You know, you're right. And your mom is probably looking at this same moon right now."

Rachel quickly looked back up and her eyes shone wet in the moonlight. Then she whispered, "I guess I'm in, then."

Belmont grinned so hard his face hurt. And then he said playfully, "Oh sorry, I couldn't hear you. Did you say something?"

"Look, I'm in. Okay?"

"What? What was that? What was that? I didn't hear anything. I'm a little tone-deaf here."

"I'm in," she said.

"Say it again."

Now yelling, "I am in!"

"Say it loud and say it proud!"

"I am in! I am in! I am IN!!"

They both laughed and high-fived.

"No. *We* are in."

Belmont helped her up and they danced a little jig in the shadow of the moon.

"Woot! Woot! We are going to do this. Look out Morge Mountain, here we come!"

They attempted another high-five but they missed and it ended in an awkward hug. The moon shone down bright, Monty had Rachel in his arms, and he felt a strange happiness.

And then from deep inside the fort, Harrison's voice yelled angrily, "Would you two coyotes please put a muzzle on it! We're trying to sleep here."

From a nice peaceful moment to the reality of The Can. It seemed strangely fitting.

Morge Mountain

Martin had stayed behind the fort to reinforce the walls and get ready for an attack if things went sour for this recovery crew.

Dante was back at Flotsam Beach. He was operating the winch that served as their transportation to, and eventual escape from, HazMat Beach.

The remaining search party had rigged three crossbars to the winching system to skurf over the lake.

Bringing up the rear, huge Magnus had nailed big leather straps onto a circular wooden dinner table where he inserted his feet. Belmont hung onto his massive waist to tag along.

In front of them, Gilly was buckled into mismatched water skis, clearly from another decade. They had tethered a belt around her waist and tied a cheap plastic sled. Apple laid in the dented toy to be pulled behind like a tow rope.

Harrison was on the lead bar with Rachael holding onto his backpack. They were both balanced on an old surfboard. They both tried to ignore the ominous bite-size chunk out of the side of the board.

Rachel came prepared for the water that she loathed so much. She had on a wetsuit – or at least half of one anyway, the upper half had been unsalvageable. While she was very careful to avoid the water spray, Rachel was actually pretty good at skurfing – much to everyone's surprise.

Now, six children hid behind an overturned ping-pong table at the edge of HazMat Beach. Each of them had the same thought: How are we going to pull this mission off?

They all stared silently and slack-jawed at what they saw before them. The group was used to mounds of trash and riffraff, but never had they seen such a threatening landscape before.

Huge rounded peaks of garbage and filth were like foothills to the ominous jagged peak behind it. In the foreground, shrouded in hazy fog, were valleys and dark paths winding through the hills of trash. Windows of darkness pockmarked the facade of the tallest mountain. Every gap in the terrain looked like a trap with teeth.

"Look at those caves," Rachel was the first to break the silence and dread hanging over the crew. "Do you think *they* live inside there?"

"Uh-Huh" was the unanimous reply. One by one they turned around and sank back down with heavy sighs.

Terrified, Belmont clutches his pitiful weapon he had brought along. It was a small slingshot made from a bungee cord stretched between an old grill fork. Dante had sewn a small leather pocket into the bungee to hold the projectile. Belmont's hand reached down to sift through the sand for something to add to the slingshot's cup in case he needed it. He came up with a double-A battery.

He stared at the battery which brought his focus back to the mission. If he could find a loose battery this easily, this mission should work. This *would* work. He pocketed the slingshot and tiny missile, and rubbed his hands together.

He paused to fidget with the spider-ring on his finger, which gave him courage. That's what this group needed right now, so he took the opportunity. He cleared his throat and found his voice.

"Okay guys, this is it. It's time we *finish* this. We know they mostly sleep during the day, and the sun will be at center in an hour. We know they can't see very well in sunlight, so we will have that advantage…and we *think* we know where the batteries are…."

Upraised eyes showing fear and exhaustion and no trace of hope all turned towards him.

"Come on guys. We can do this."

Harry snorted but there wasn't much effort in it.

"Sure we can. Listen. We're fast. And we can scrabble like monkeys. They couldn't catch us, even if they *did* wake up. Do you know why? Because we have these."

He thrust his fist forward and his small orange plastic spider ring shone like a beacon of strength. One by one they all thrust their fists forwards and smiled nodding at Belmont.

"We've got a great plan to get out of here," Harrison grinned warmly at Belmont. "Let's go knock 'em dead!"

The Lair

Gilly was to keep the skurfboards, skis, and various T-bar and winch accessories safe. They left her at the beach nervously wading in the shallow water and holding the lines ready for a quick escape.

The other five JYKs trudged past the trash wall dividing the beach from the paths that lead to Morge Mountain. When they came to the edge of the mountain of trash, they all peered up to the summit.

"How far do you think we need to climb up?" Belmont asked, knowing none of them had the answer.

"Probably not far, they won't like it closer to the lights – I hope." Harrison replied.

"Okay, here's where Magnus and Apple stay behind. We need you to keep a close eye for us or Morges – or *us* being *chased* by Morges. Magnus, you're our last line of defense. If they are after us, we need you to, um, *interrupt* the chase." Rachel ended, not really knowing how to say, "Fight a monster."

Magnus slammed his giant iron club into his open palm, and gave a mean look. Then he smiled warmly at Rachel and hugged her close.

"Oof! Do that again, and you'll need to fight me." She said, unconvincingly.

"You know what, I can climb super fasty-fast. Fasty than Belmonty. I'm gonna come." Apple chimed in.

"No. You have the most important job. You need to watch for us, as soon as you see us, run and tell Magnus to get ready and then sprint back to tell Gilly. Got it?"

Apple didn't look convinced, so Belmont leaned in close to whisper, "Honestly, Magnus is a little afraid and he needs you to keep watch. Can you help protect Magnus?"

That seemed to brighten her up. "Fine, but don't 'spect me to come finding you if you're in trubby-ble."

Harry, Rachel and Belmont climbed in through the low small cave and were immediately plunged into darkness. The dank smell of motor oil, rust and something animalistic was everywhere. Rachel pulled her shirt over her face to lessen the impact.

They climbed on their hands and knees for what seemed like forever. They were heading gradually upwards at an angle and the tunnel was slowly widening so they no longer needed to crawl. Slumping hunch-backed through a wide turn in the corridor, they came to a blocked passage with a rusted ladder leaning heavily on the wall.

"I guess we go upward and onward," Belmont managed.

"Great. It's starting to smell worse, if that's possible."

And it was. It was no longer just a lingering greasy smell, but now it was a harsh, sharp smell that made their eyes water.

"Come on ya wimps." Rachel muffled through her shirt. She was the first to grab the ladder and climb up into the dark.

"After you," said Harry and then followed quickly behind Belmont.

They climbed for about two stories and then came out into a larger passage. To the left of them, they could see some light shining through the nooks and crannies of the garbage that made up the face of the mountain. At the end of the passage towards the face was an opening into an orange garbage can that seemed to provide an alternative tunnel out of the place. They looked longingly at the tunnel and light, wishing they could go that direction.

"We're not going that way. We've got to go in farther." Rachel said, as she helped Belmont turn his gaze back to the right.

They tiptoed down the passage until they came to a shelf of trash before a large cavern.

"Shhh. Get down." Rachel hissed as she pulled at the boys' arms. Both of them slumped heavily against the shelf. "I heard something in there."

They all got close to the shelf and peeked their heads over.

"I can't *see* anything. But I do think I hear something. Wait. I see something very shiny in the way back. Give me the flashlight," Harry was squinting into the dark.

They had found a tiny penlight that had surprisingly worked. It had just a very narrow beam, and a rather dull one, at that. But they coveted the working light like a thirsty man covets his last drops of water.

Rachel clicked on the dull light and handed it carefully to Harry.

"I can barely see... oh my, oh my. There they are. There they are!" His whisper got louder as he got more excited.

Both Belmont and Rachel sat up and looked over the edge. They saw a tall pile of batteries lying on the far end of the cave. There must have been hundreds. Black, silvery, square, rectangle, cylindrical. All shapes and sizes and versions. There even seemed to be some car batteries thrown in.

Harrison mouthed a loud but silent "Yes" to his comrades. But before they could celebrate, the beam of light touched on a clawed foot laying directly in front of the pile. Harry slowly arced the light up the foot and found it was attached to a powerful hairy leg which was then attached to a ferocious, but sleeping Morge.

Their eyes grew wide with panic as the light continued across the cavern floor and they saw another clawed foot. And then a long arm. And then the heaving chest of another Morge, and another and another.

"There must be a dozen... or more," Belmont whispered.

Rachel yanked him back down. "Okay guys, look at me and focus..."

Belmont sat down and Harry squatted to listen.

"Here's the plan. These guys are asleep. We can sneak by them, fill the backpack up with batteries and sneak back."

"That's not a plan. That's just stupidity!" Harry hissed back.

"I don't see you with any better ideas... what in the *gravy* is that awful smell??" Rachel pushed back from the two boys and covered her mouth.

Harry looked guilty, but then the smell overcame him and he also jumped back a few feet gagging, "Oh man that is *nasty*."

"I'm not sure I smell anything new. Oh gosh, there it is. Yep, that's awful. Where is it coming from..." Belmont looked around him and patted his body down. As he got to his backside, he grimaced as he felt something muddy and wet. He brought his hand up to his face and was overpowered by the smell.

"Oh no! I sat in something," he gagged.

"What the muck? You sat in a Morge toilet?"

Monty got dizzy and slumped forward on his knees and immediately regretted the move. "Oh man, now I *knelt* in something, too."

"Dude!" Harrison barked.

"*Shh!* They can hear you." Rachel shushed.

"Don't worry. They'll *smell* him first," Harry snapped, looking at Monty as he wiped his hands on his now putrid sweater and pants. "You smell almost as bad as them," he hooked a finger towards the lair.

"Truly. Wait, that's right. You really do. Honestly, that's a great idea! That's it. Belmont, you sneak in there smelling as bad as you are, and they'll think you're one of them." Rachel clapped her hands softly together.

"I don't know about that. That seems a little, ah, dangerous." Belmont shifted uncomfortably.

"Maybe, but remember, they're all asleep anyway. Your terrible, terrible, *terrible* smell won't wake them. Probably."

A few moments later, Belmont was tiptoeing through the large cavern with sleeping monsters on either side of him. Harrison kept the flashlight on a low beam and pointed down the aisle. Monty tried to remain focused on the battery pile not far ahead of him through the channel of sleeping death to either side.

"See, it works." Rachel stage-whispers to him.

"Yeah, maybe she's right. It is working," he says to himself.

"Keep going big guy, you got this." As Harry offered his words of encouragement, he accidentally slid the flashlight switch from low beam to high. A piercing beam of light dragged across the huge hairy chest of a Morge and then up to its upturned face.

"Turn that off," Rachel hissed. She reached for it, but Harry pulled it back. The movement caused the beam to slide up the beast's chest and lock onto its terrible eyes.

"I got it!" and he flicked the light off. The beast's face returned to shadow and the cavern is plunged into darkness.

Belmont blinked hard, trying to erase the halos in his eyes from the temporary wash of light. His foot had stopped in mid step and he slowly placed it down into the darkness. No contact was made with any unnatural object, so he slowly moved his other foot forward.

Inch by painful inch, Belmont made his way to the battery pile. He quietly opened the red backpack that Harrison had given him and scooped up a massive load of batteries. For good measure, he grabbed a few rectangular batteries and stuffed them into various pockets.

"I think I hear one waking up." Rachel whispered.

"Really? Where??" Monty stood up quickly and started to tiptoe back towards where Rachel and Harrison were hiding.

She yanked the flashlight from Harry and flicked it on high. The light cast a beam directly on the broad shoulders of a standing Morge peering down at Monty, who was eyeball to hairy eyeball with the massive beast.

The Morge stared blankly and gave a sniff. Belmont stood stock still while the monster's eyes pivoted on their stalks. The beast uttered a low growl and smelled him again.

Over its giant shoulder, Belmont could see movement by Harry. He was reaching his arm back and had something in his palm. Sensing that something terrible was about to happen, Belmont closed his eyes and held his breath.

Harry chucked an apple with all the power of a pony-league pitcher. It made immediate contact with the creature's head and smashed to a pulp. The impact slowly resonated with the beast, and it turned in the direction of the cowering children. But its eyes wobbled on their stalks and lingered a moment squarely on Monty. Slowly one eye swung around and then the other to stare at the two faces peeking above their hiding spot.

While the monster's gaze turned fully towards its attackers, Belmont sensed an opportunity and quickly slid to the other side of the aisle. He was trying to use the beast's massive size to his advantage, but just as Monty was around the monster, it whipped back around. Suddenly, it swung its long arms towards Belmont intending to scoop him up.

Monty ducked the colossal talons and broke into a sprint towards the opening. The beast hesitated for just a moment, still confused by sleep and the dancing flashlight beam. But it recovered and let out a tremendous howl.

"Run!!" Shouted Belmont as he passed them. But he didn't have to say it twice. Harry and Rachel were already scrambling towards the exit ladder that they had climbed earlier by the time Belmont was on the ground below.

The Monster leaped the shelf they were hiding under in a single terrifying bound, and reached towards the kids. Its claws made slight contact with Rachel and made a tear in her shirt. But its focus was on the bouncing beam of the flashlight. Its second arm reached farther and snatched the device from her hands. It stopped in mid stride, claws screeching against the flooring of the tunnel, to gnash the tiny light between its teeth. The flashlight shattered loudly and pieces fell around its feet.

The light extinguished, the beast stared back at the kids getting away down the corridors. It let out another predatory howl which pierced their eardrums.

Belmont chanced a look over his shoulder as he approached the end of the tunnel. That's when he saw a dozen Morges hopping down the ladder into the narrow corridor behind the lead beast.

"We're done for" was his first thought. "We'll never make it out this way…"
Flee!

"No time for the other ladder. Follow me!"

Belmont's eyes caught the orange glow coming from the waste can hanging off to the side. Nothing could be seen of the end, and he hoped it was what he thought it was.

He cut across the tunnel and dove into the mouth of the orange can. He slammed into the hard plastic, and then fell out of view through the back.

Harrison and Rachel exchanged a half glance and both jumped towards the chute; Rachel made the dive a half second before Harry.

As Belmont had hoped, they were in an old construction chute used to drip garbage from tall sites. It framed a slide that dropped for about three floors before starting to twist outward from the mountain.

As Belmont tossed and tumbled through the tunnel, at one point he had a sickeningly awkward angle of staring backwards up the tunnel through his feet. He saw a shock of long brown hair falling rapidly towards him.

Seconds later, Belmont belly-flopped on the roof of a rusted trucking container with a loud grunt. "Uumph!"

He repeated the grunt as Rachel landed on top of him, feet-to-head. "Oof!"

She jarred her chin into his butt cheek and grimaced as the wet muck on Belmont's pants smeared her face.

"Hnnuoof!" Belmont grunted a third time, as Harrison landed hard in a sitting position on top of the both of them. Rachel's face again connected with Belmont's butt; this time entirely awash in the slime.

The three of them paused for a second on the roof of the van. Harrison looked up through the bottom of the chute dangling above him.

"Well, that's one way to…"

His words were cut off as the rusty roof suddenly collapsed inward.

Layered on top of each other on a rusty patch of metal, they fell into the shipping container. The sheet of metal from the roof formed a sort of sled and jettisoned them out of the back of the van like a toboggan leaving a starting gate.

The doors kicked open and the makeshift sled barreled out. It went airborne for seconds before the landing on the side of the dangerously slanting mountain wall.

The sled hit hard. Rachel's foot bounced and kicked Harry in the nose, making his eyes well up and his vision cloud over with tears. He heard Rachel yell sorry, but then feels her bounce and whiplash forward to clock her forehead against the sled bottom between Belmont's ankles. With his vision blurry, all Harry could see is a watery view of the horizon slanted crazily in front of them.

They careen down the slope as a crazy three-layer mess. First, Belmont on the bottom facing forward, but not able to lift his head for the weight on top of him. Rachel sandwiched in the middle facing backwards with her head between Belmont's knees and Harry is perched shakily on top; facing forward as though he's riding a bucking bronco.

Harry saw that the sled was zooming down towards a large drop and he leaned heavily left. This changed their course a bit to avoid the cliff. But they connect with a car hood and launch off another three feet below. They land hard again, and Harry's face connects with the back of Belmont's head. He tastes blood and a grittiness that he assumes is part of a tooth.

They continue their descent with Harry shifting irregularly to avoid particularly rigid mounds of rubble and trash. Soon, he regrets a move as they plummet towards a low half-arch of broken concrete.

Recognizing they wouldn't make the turn, he leaned as far back as he could into full limbo mode and barely snuck under. While they plummeted underneath the cement tunnel, Harry's nose dragged on the underside of the cement arch and singed the skin down to a raw blister. He popped up once they got out from under the tunnel and a thin stream of smoke trailed from his nose.

"Oww-sheesh!" he cried and grabbed his face, but it was much too sore. He didn't have time to dwell on the issue, as the flat bottom of the mountain was quickly approaching them.

The juncture of the hill caused a sharp angle with the ground. Harry quickly ripped off his belt to lasso it forward. The belt caught underneath, but the leather strap went taught and smacked Belmont in the face.

"Ouch."

Harry pulled hard at the belt and managed to bring the front of the sled to a toboggan-like curve. Meanwhile, Rachel dangled her backpack straps off the back of the sled and let them drag as an anchor.

Just as the sled connected with the plateau of flat ground below, Rachel's homemade anchor caught and stopped the sled dead. The three travelers immediately slid off the sled and continued to ride Belmont through a mud slick for a few feet. They came to rest a few inches from a bubbling pit of tar.

The sudden stillness was interrupted by Apple, "Woo-wee. That was Amazy-mazing. I want to do it."

There was Rachel lying backwards on top of Belmont, her face framed in now dried Morge slime. Harry sat astride them both with a belt reign in his hand. He looked a bit like Santa; complete with a red – albeit still smoking, nose.

The three of them looked back up the mountain of chaos they just came down and then back to Apple. Then back up at the mountain.

A moment passed and then a chorus of guttural shrieks pierced the stillness. Far up the mountain, a black mass of bodies emerged from the holes in the face of the mountain and started bearing down the mountain.

Apple took off running down the path, executing her role in this terrible mission.

"Magnus. Gilly. Here they COME!" she was shouting.

"I hope you got the batteries." Rachel said, getting up from the sled-sandwich she was part of.

Monty stared dumbfounded and then frantically searched for the backpack as he recovered.

"GOT IT!" Monty shouted proudly, and held up the tattered backpack.

"Great. Now RUN!!" Rachel screamed. And they did.

They found themselves fleeing down the same valley that they had come up. This time, there was no need for stealth, just speed.

Belmont found himself in the back behind Rachel. He could see Apple far down the path sprinting like a gazelle. Not for the first time, he was surprised by her speed and agility. But he didn't have time to think about it. Behind him he could hear the howls of the charging Morge tribe.

Fortunately, they had a healthy head-start on the troop. And, as expected, the beasts did not seem to be as fast in the bright sunlight that lit the floor of The Can. But they were plenty fast enough. And mad... not just mad; enraged!

And as quick as the kids were, the tribe was gaining on them.

"Here's the halfway point," Harrison shouted as he passed Belmont in the foot race. He quickly pointed at the slanted bench and upturned table they rested at just a few short hours ago.

"Only half?" Belmont groaned.

Rachel looked back with a grim smile, "So I guess we know which is a glass-half-full and glass-half-empty type person."

The lead Morge was gaining on them. It was smaller than most, but obviously faster. It was a silvery gray mass of sharp teeth and claws.

The beast would stretch its long arms forward, plant them and then swing its squat body to land on its stubby feat.

Belmont smelled it coming first. It smelled like rotten fish, but burned his nostrils like bleach.

He heard the scrabble of gravel and the thump of its stubby feet on the path. He knew a few more strides and the monster would be on top of him.

Thump... Scrabble. Once.

Thump... Scrabble. Twice.

Thump... Scrabble. Three times.

Monty winced in mid-stride. He felt massive arms embrace him. They felt like an iron vice around his arms, crushing them to his sides. It hoisted him up and over and onto its shoulders and he lost his breath as he banged hard against its massive back.

Through squeezed eyes he couldn't see, but he heard the awful scream from the beast.

He knew he was a goner.

But something didn't make sense. Why did the scream come from behind him? And why was he continuing to move forward? Monty squinted an eye open and peeked over his own shoulder to look at the monster.

To his relief, he saw the massive blond head of Magnus.

Magnus turned his head towards Belmont and winked.

Magnus had picked up Belmont at the very last minute and gave him an extra boost. He was being carried, firemen style, as Magnus ran through the valley.

"Oh thank God. He almost ate me." Belmont let his gaze go backwards over Magnus's shoulder. And came face-to-face with the gnashing beast. Its razor teeth clamped down inches from Belmont's nose.

It missed, fell a few steps behind Magnus's massive strides, but quickly gained again as it swung its body towards him. As it leapt forward again, it gnashed its teeth at Belmont's face. This time, Belmont smelled its hot breath, and felt its bristly hair on his nose.

Belmont knew the next lunge would end badly. Monty squirmed one arm loose from Magnus's grip and found he was holding the slingshot that had been in his back pocket. In one motion, he grabbed the bungee with his teeth, felt the battery in the cup, and outstretched his free arm.

He opened his teeth and let the band snap. The battery shot like a bullet towards the Morge. The monster leapt with open jaws to gouge Monty's face. But the missile found its mark squarely in the back of the beast's throat.

The tubular eyes bulged out. Its leap was drawn short and its howl ended in a gasping choke. The monster fell in a silver mess of fur and limbs and immediately started to claw at its throat. The kids pulled ahead, and Magnus lowered Belmont down to the ground. Belmont fell in stride right beside him.

Belmont almost cried out when he saw the beach immediately in front of them and noticed no other beast had yet caught up. Gilly was standing in the shallow water holding one of the tow ropes and steadying the homemade skurfboards. Her feet were already in her mismatched skis, and her buddy belt was hanging behind her on top of the sled.

"Hurry!" she screamed. Harrison was first onto his board. Gilly gave him the T-bar and Rachel grabbed his backpack. She then leaned over and helped Apple lay in the sled and grab hold of the belt hanging behind Gilly.

Magnus stepped onto the table top with Belmont close behind him. Belmont hooked his hands in Magnus's belt. All three tagalongs – Rachel, Apple and Belmont – raised their arms and stuck their thumbs into the air, and hoped Dante had seen them.

Skurf or Die!

There was a brief pause, barely a few seconds, while nothing happened. But in that short time, five Morges charged the beach screaming their war cry. They saw the group in the water and started to slowly circle the shoreline. The moment was tense as one waded in, baring its fangs and dragging its claws in the water.

All of a sudden, the winch kicked in aggressively. The group shot forward onto the water with a jarring start. All three teams staggered in their footholds and Magnus almost tumbled in, but they all regained their balance and skied out into open water.

At the last moment, an exceptionally large Morge got a long claw on Apple's shoe. The shoe immediately pulled off and the beast fell face first in the water, but the impact knocked Apple off-balance.

She screamed and rolled off the sled. The cheap plastic toy scooted out from under her and bobbed worthlessly away. Apple held onto the tow rope, but now was completely laying on the water getting dragged behind. She was dunked twice and the water got up her nose. She rolled onto her back for a second and it allowed them to get a little bit of a distance from the beach. But everyone knew she would not be able to hang on much longer. As the group skidded across the water picking up speed, Apple bounced hard against the choppy water.

"Help!" she screamed, and then swallowed a gulp of water. She tried to yell again, but ended up coughing and choking.

And then it happened… She let go! The group quickly left her in their wake as she splashed helplessly in the open water.

Belmont was the first to see it. "Oh no, we lost her. We lost Apple!"

Rachel turned around and spotted her. She lost her balance a bit and then steadied herself. She stared ahead for a moment lost in thought, and then seemed to make up her mind. She made eye contact with Belmont, who sensed what she was about to do.

"No! Don't do it. You can't swim!"

And that's when she let go of the backpack. Rachel leaned to the side of her surfboard and half fell, half dived into the water. And then disappeared under the surface.

The group continued to jet across the water towards the safety of the far shore. As they found themselves halfway across the lake, Belmont saw Rachel's wetsuit float to the surface.

Being the only one dragging behind a skier, Belmont was able to see this but the rest were focused on looking ahead.

"Rachel's gone, too. Oh no, Rachel and Apple are both gone!"

To make matters worse, Belmont could just barely make out a few Morges swimming out towards Apple.

"We have to go back," Belmont yelled.

"We can't until we get across to the other side. It doesn't go in reverse."

"We need to go back around then."

"I don't know if I can make it. I'm so tired already," Gilly said.

Belmont could tell Gilly was barely hanging on, and Harrison didn't seem much better. Even Magnus seemed under strain from dragging his enormous bulk across the water after such a fast sprint from the monsters.

"No you can't. But I can…. I'm still fresh and I can make it back in time."

"But you can't save them."

"I need to try. No, strike that. I *need* to save them."

As the far beach came into view, Belmont scooted underneath Magnus's legs and squatted in front of him. He grabbed the tow handle inside of Magnus's grip.

"What will you do for skis?" Gilly asked loudly, to make her voice heard over the winch and water spray. "You can't use the table like Magnus."

Almost before she finished, Harrison took a sharp edge on his modified wake board and shot towards Magnus's skiff. He timed it perfectly and gingerly stepped off while keeping his balance. "Good luck. Bring them back – please."

Harry pushed the board up onto the moving raft, and fell back into the water. Without missing a beat, Monty stepped onto the board and stood forward. The board took to the water in front of Magnus. Belmont gently peeled Magnus's grip from the handle and let him fall back into the water. By now they were safely in shallow water approaching the little cove that they had left a couple of hours ago.

Gilly rode her skis right up on the sand and collapsed forward. Behind her, Magnus and Harry were wading up to the shore. All of them were spent.

Belmont turned a hard edge in the water. The winch line spun through the turnstile and sprang back out over the water. Belmont took to the lake and shot past Magnus and Harry. He focused his eyes and spotted Apple still splashing across the lake. Even harder to see were the long arms of the Morges paddling towards Apple.

But something seemed off. It seemed like Apple was swimming towards Belmont at a very fast pace. While Apple was a decent swimmer, she seemed to be cruising at an unnatural pace.

Belmont and Apple were quickly approaching each other. Apple was moving so fast she was causing a wake of waves behind her.

"Whaaaa?" he whispered to himself. And then he saw a green scaled fin pop up in the water behind her.

"What the fish?"

Meanwhile, Harrison and Magnus waded up to the beach where Gilly was lying in the sand on her back. Dante leaned out of the winch operator seat with questions written all over his face.

"Morges attacked. Apple fell. Rachel jumped in after her. Monty going back to save them." Harrison panted and then collapsed on the sand next to Gilly. Skiing was tiring. Skiing while pulling someone behind you – after running from attacking monsters – was purely exhausting.

"*Odio decir esto, pero no puedes descansar ahora. ¡Mirar!*"

Dante was pointing at the far shore and arching his arm towards the water bridges over the rapids that separated the lakes. No one had their eyes open, let alone were paying attention, so he tried again.

"*¿Me has oído? ¡Vienen!*"

And then he yelled…"Morges!"

At that, three pairs of eyes snapped open and looked at what Dante was pointing at. About a dozen or so Morges were running down shore towards the water bridges. Some had already reached the beginning and were starting to make their way across.

"Oh great, now don't they know that's not safe." Gilly said, exacerbated. She looked out across the water towards Belmont and Apple. "Oh. If those guys come back, the Morges might be here waiting for them. We have to stop them."

"Or, lead them away." Harrison finished. "We need to lead them away and then circle back to the fort. When we get there, hopefully Martin will have made sure everything is in order in case we need to defend it."

"Dante, you stay there in the winch seat. You know how to operate it, and they may need help when they get back."

While the three wet and tired kids started off towards the rapids, Dante nodded, and shifted back into the operator seat. He peered through the mounted binoculars and gaped at what he saw across the lake.

Meanwhile, Monty was buzzing along at a good clip towards the other side. Strangely, Apple was buzzing towards him at an even faster pace. He again saw the green scaled tail splash behind Apple and was concerned that Apple was being attacked by some large fish. But she seemed to be enjoying the ride. In fact, as she was approaching Monty at an unbelievable pace. He saw her smiling and singing, "Weeeee, I'm a flying fish. Weeeee, I'm a flying fish."

Apple was coming closer and they were about to pass each other. She was so fast that she was causing a wake of waves that Monty had to ride through.

"Hi Belmonty. I'm a flying fish."

"I see! But how are you doing that?!" Monty yelled back as they passed each other.

Apple buzzed by and he got a glimpse of something in the water that she was sort of riding. It seemed to be *two somethings* because he glimpsed two slender fish tails swimming furiously just beneath the surface.

Apple was now heading in the other direction and they were separating quickly.

"What are you riding on?" He yelled.

Apple yelled back, but Monty could no longer hear over the sound of the splashing waves, the winch line and the growing distance between them.

Unfortunately, Monty did not have much time to dwell on the issue as he had another problem. He was heading directly for hostile territory. A few dozen yards away, some of the Morges that swam after Apple were still in the water. The winch line was taking him directly into their path.

"Oh *shiitake*!" he said and steadied the board for some drastic moves. Belmont was no beginner, but he never had to avoid angry monsters in the water before. He was a little nervous to say the least. But he carved expertly around one of them and quickly skirted around another. And then he threaded his way between two nasty black ones that clawed the water at him.

There was one last one he was approaching that was bigger and slower than the rest. It seemed to be struggling to stay afloat. Monty went right over his head, and stomped the board down hard for good measure. He turned around and saw to his satisfaction that the Morge sank beneath the water.

Belmont was again approaching the shore he seemingly just left, but there were no longer any waiting monsters. They had either swum out to get Apple, or had run down the shore towards the bridges.

But Monty was not focused on this issue. His heart leapt in his throat as he saw the red backpack lying in the shallow water. In all of the commotion, he hadn't even noticed he had lost it. As the towline spun through the winch cog, Monty angled hard towards the backpack, grabbed it and put it on in one motion. The line went slack a bit and then came back around swiftly.

"Here we go again," he said to himself and shot back out towards the open water.

For the second time in as many minutes, he plowed towards the swimming Morges. They seemed baffled as to which direction to swim. He clumped another one on the head and watched it sink beneath the surface. The rest of the way was clear, and he focused his attention on the small dot of Apple on the other shore. And there was someone else with her.

Fish Tale

As Monty approached the shore, Apple was flapping her arms while run-splashing in the shallows yelling, "Zoom, I'm a flying fish…. Wee!"

And nearby, half submerged in the shallow water – her hair lying wet on her shoulders, Rachel smiled shyly.

"Hiya, Belmont."

"Rachel?! You *swam*?! I saw you sink. You can't swim, but you saved her. You… whaaa…" Monty trailed off as a fin appeared behind Rachel in the water followed by another one.

"What the What!?!"

Dante came down from the winch seat with his mouth hanging open almost to his chest with surprise.

Rachel popped up, revealing two sleek legs covered in greenish scales. Each leg ended in a slender fin that splayed out a bit when she stepped down. Two more fins flanked her shins, flaring out as they moved down from her knee towards her ankle. She had another two shorter ones, although thicker, on the side of her thighs ending just below her damp shorts.

"Rachel. You. Ah. Yer. You're…"

"You're pretty," Apple giggled.

"Yes, but…" Belmont stammered.

"But?? 'But' what??" Rachel snapped.

"Sorry, not 'but'. 'And'… You're pretty AND…a mermaid."

"That's right. And this mermaid's going to kick your butt if you don't stop staring…" she trailed off as she looked over Belmont's shoulder towards the lake.

"Change that. Stare all you want, but do it while you…RUN!"

Belmont and Dante broke their stare at Rachel's strange, but oddly normal, legs and turned to look.

A half dozen ravaging beasts were scurrying across the safety bridges and getting very close to shore.

Belmont stumbled as he tried to run without first getting out of the skurf boots. He kicked them free and sprinted to catch up with the group.

Apple had a head start on them and was racing far ahead. Dante was in front of Rachel, who was running awkwardly because of her mini fins. Belmont caught up quickly and said in between breaths, "I hope Martin was able to set up the defense like we planned."

A moment later Rachel's skin faded to her natural coloring and the fins seemed to shrink into her feet. She was soon outpacing Belmont, yet again.

"Keep up," she snapped, and then pulled quickly ahead.

Attack

They raced in the direction of the fort and heard the howling tribe getting closer behind them. The sun was just dipping below the horizon and they would soon be plunged into darkness until the safety lights came on. From a few hundred yards down the trail they saw the others clamoring towards the fort.

"The Morges crossed the bridge," Harry was in the lead waving and shouting to Martin, who was on a perch of a bent flagpole high above the face of the mound.

"Get in here! But, be careful where you step. I've made some modifications. A wrong step would be very…something, something." Martin called down to the approaching group.

"We double-backed around and think we lost them back at the bridge, but I don't think it will be long before they…"

Gilly, Magnus and the rest were standing on the path before the muck-path staring down the trail when Apple busted through the car door-gate that opened to the path.

"Apple. Oh, Jeepers! You made it. Belmont saved you!" Gilly clapped her hands together when they ran by.

"No he didn't. You know what, I'm a flying fish…" and she flapped her arms as she ran by them down the path and hopscotched her way across the rubble-path towards the fort.

Dante came through next and shouted something in Spanish, and also raced across the muck-path. Martin shouted down to him to be careful but hurry up. Dante had some words for him back, and they didn't sound that friendly.

Rachel busted through the gate and Gilly clapped again. "Oh, Belmont saved you too. Yay!"

"Not even close." Rachel growled, but she didn't stop to argue. She charged towards the fort and sprang over the first two stepping crates to land on the submerged hood of a car. "And get moving, or else you'll need saving."

Belmont came through the door looking exhausted and ready to puke. He staggered toward Magnus, and collapsed. Magnus reached down and picked him up by the belt and started to walk over the muck-path.

Suddenly, the car door gate burst from its hinge and a foaming, frothing, snarling, angry Morge leapt through the gate. A smaller rust color one soon followed as they both looked around for their prey.

"Get in here," Martin yelled to the others from one of the fort's "windows", which was actually a doorless refrigerator. The Morges heard his voice and howled as they charged toward the fort from the side, heedless of the muck that lay in between them and their prey.

The smaller one reached the muck first and bounded in. It fell face first as its feet hit the mucky pond and it started to sink slowly into the ooze. As the back of its head started to submerge, a brown MugSlug encircled it and helped bring him down under the surface. The beast disappeared with a muddy burp.

The large Morge was able to keep its balance, but soon was mired knee-deep in brownish mucusy substance. It could no longer move forward and started to sink to its thighs. The beast growled and swung its massive arms out to grab a broken chair poking above the surface. At the same time, a MugSlug encircled its wrist and started to pull the huge hand under. Another slug, and then another started to slip around its torso pulling it down into the depths. The beast sank faster as slugs wormed up from the sludge and pulled it deeper. The ooze covered its chest, then neck and then chin. The Morge never looked panicked, but instead snarled and bit at the mud and worms. Its face slowly submerged as a fat rust-colored slug slunk over its eyes and pulled the monster under completely.

As these two beasts succumbed to MucLake, another six crashed through the gate. They stood watching their pack mates' demise, and it seemed to take some of the zeal out of their charge. They gave the lake a respectful distance which allowed the JYKs some much needed time to get across the path.

But the pause was short lived. The monsters warily approached the edge of the muck with their terrible mouths dripping with saliva and claws ripping at the air in front of them.

A Morge spotted Belmont swinging across the rusted ladder halfway across to the fort and it inflamed the beast. It shrieked and leapt with its powerfully stout legs, making it to the hood of the car in one bound. Its claws skittered on the smooth metal as one foot slipped into the muck.

Immediately, it pulled it out but a MugSlug had already leached onto the hairy paw. The beast growled as it ripped the slimy green slug off of its foot and gnashed it between its teeth in anger.

The remaining five Morges, emboldened by their leader, started to hop from each rubble step-stone to the next, leapfrogging their way to the fort.

The leader leapt again towards the monkey-bar ladder and swung easily through. The contraption groaned under its weight but the beast landed heavily on the other side and started to clamber up the wall of the fort.

Martin blared his trumpet (significantly off key), and released a lever. A huge barrel rolled out from an outcropping of rubbish, and fell hard, spilling nails and bits of metal as it spun towards the Morge. Then, with a tremendous BASH! The barrel connected with the Morge's upturned face.

The barrel shattered and metal debris rained down the beast's face and chest. The JYKs let out a collective cheer as the beast staggered backward and knocked into a Morge that had quickly followed behind. The second one fell to its end.

But the cheering died as the first Morge regained its balance and lifted its bloody face. One loose fang fell from its jaw as it snarled up at them. The tooth hit the platform the beast was standing on with a slight TOCK.

The animal let out an awful roar, but was cut off suddenly as the outcropping gave way, and the beast fell with a small avalanche of trash. It landed on its back in the ooze, and immediately disappeared under a small mountain of loose rubble from the fort walls. The trash, and presumably the monster below it, sank beneath the surface a few moments later.

Quickly, two other Morges replaced their leader as they swung through the ladder maze. The first one landed on the slide and slipped to the bottom where it held on momentarily before falling into the swamp with a squelchy PLOP!

The second one landed on the back of the first and leapfrogged onto the wall of the fort.

Immediately, a spring loaded dumpster door slammed open and knocked the Morge straight down into the brown sludge below. It landed flat footed and crumpled completely unconscious. The slugs and the muck did the rest.

Another Morge struggled to the slide and swung across to the main fort wall, quickly scrambling over the trap door and up towards the top. Another spring door snapped open, but the Morge dodged it and grabbed hold of the door, hoisting itself up.

As it rose to its full height, it came eye to eye with another huge beast standing at the top of the fort. This one hairless, but no less intimidating…

Magnus stood armed with a steel post at the top of the fort's wall. He stared unblinking into the ferocious orbs of the Morge. Magnus grinned a toothy smile as the Morge opened its jaws to scream in his face.

The beast raised its long claws to tear the throat of its adversary. Magnus raised the club, but it appeared to be a moment too late.

But just at that moment, Apple appeared at the beast's knee and shouted, "No No, Morgy Morge. You will not hurt Magny-pie. Bye-bye now." And she yanked the bolt from the door hinge.

The monster looked down for a split second before the door collapsed downward. At the same time, Magnus brought the pole down on top of its head.

With a Crack, the beast fell straight down and landed flat footed in the muck. It slowly sank beneath the surface in a slow boil of brown/green bubbles.

One lone Morge remained pacing aggressively back and forth on the fringe of MucLake as it witnessed the last of its pack sink beneath the surface. It studied the fort area and caught Belmont's eye. It stared unblinking for a long moment. Then it snarled loudly, turned and leapt back up the trail.

Cell Charge

The JYKs all scrambled from their various hiding places and battle stations to Glen. Sparks was there cowering under a crate, but wagged his tail tentatively when the kids formed a semi circle around Magma.

"Is everyone okay?" Martin asked.

Surprised by the simple question, each one of them looked questioningly at him. Then they immediately started to take stock of the situation. They looked at themselves, patted down their torsos to make sure they weren't injured, and then looked at each other before answering simultaneously.

"I think so."

"Gosh, yes."

"Surprisingly – yeah."

"Yeah, of course."

"You know what, yesyes."

"Si. Si."

They paused a moment more before Rachel said, "Well? Did we do it? Did we get the batteries?"

Belmont, remembering the backpack, shook it off and held it high. "Yes we did!" he exclaimed.

The group immediately started to embrace each other in celebration. Some were crying joyfully, others were continuing to pat their friends down and making sure they weren't injured.

Belmont threw the backpack down and they all stared at it silently. They looked at each other wide-eyed and slack-jawed. Were they really in possession of something that could save them? Was there magic in that backpack? Everyone was afraid to look and possibly shatter the hope that they had embraced.

Harry was the first to break the silence. "They're in there." It was somewhere between a statement and a question.

"Yeah I think so, I mean I hope so." Belmont said.

"You think so?! You hope so?!" Rachel barked, back to her old self now that the silent spell had been broken.

"Yeah, well a lot has happened since I, you know, stuffed them in there!" Belmont defended.

"Fair enough," she relented. "Well, let's see what we got."

Dante was closest and leaned down to put his hands on the bag. He hesitated and looked up at the group for support. As one, they all inhaled a breath. He looked back down and unzipped the bag slowly; the clicking zipper teeth unnerved the group.

"Come on, get on with it! You're killing me here!" Shouted the typically meek Gilly.

He finished by tearing open the bag and spilling its contents all over the ground. Black rectangles of all sizes were scattered everywhere, and here and there large silver cylinders rolled away from the bag.

"Well, there we go. Batteries!" Harry said.

"Yeah, I didn't really know what kind we needed so I grabbed a bunch of different kinds. I hope…"

"Belmonty, you did awesomely awesome." Apple sang. "That's more batty-ries than I've ever seen."

"All we need is one." Martin said.

"Yes, but we need one that works. Get the phone. Let's do this."

A duck-taped shoe box was brought carefully from a hiding place. Inside the box, a gym towel was wrapped tightly around a slightly smaller box. In turn, this box held a bubble-wrapped package. Finally, the phone emerged in a zip-locked plastic baggie. A tiny little pink bell, like you'd find on a cat's collar, hung from the phone.

Belmont looked up at Gilly with a smile.

"Well, I didn't want it to get dropped. Or wet. Or lost." Gilly said embarrassed.

The search for a fitting battery started immediately. They would rifle through the pile of black squares and rectangles, and pass one back to Belmont as they found a promising sign.

At first, they seemed to try them all. But they got more and more selective as, through trial and error, they knew what not to look for.

Soon they were down to a handful when Dante perked up. "This is it. I can tell. Same size, same number of prongs. This is it."

They all stopped as he held it up and passed it hand-over-hand to Belmont who inspected it.

"That's it," said Martin.

"Batty battery," said Apple.

"Eek! I can feel it." Squeaked Gilly.

Belmont laid the black rectangle over the cell phone. The size seemed about right but it laid on top and wobbled.

"Remember, it won't be charged so it won't work yet." Harry said.

Belmont pushed gently but firmly down with one finger. They held their breath. And then "Click", the battery snapped into place.

"Belmonty did it!" Apple chimed.

"Not so fast. Does it work?" Rachel asked anxiously.

All sets of eyes stared at the screen. One second, two seconds… Then five more.

"It wasn't going to be charged, I told you so." Harry said. "Of course not, right?"

"That's okay. We planned for this. Come here." Martin said.

Dante ran ahead, chatting as he approached a long cord hanging from… the sky?

"Whaa…?"

"Lookie, it comes from the Moony." Apple said.

"It almost seems to." Rachel agreed.

"Not quite. See, it's quite amazing. I came up with this idea…" Martin started.

"*¿Acabas de tomar todo el crédito?*" Dante snapped at Martin.

"Okay…WE had this awesome idea. We didn't really think climbing Morge Mountain to the lighting grid was a smart idea – no offense Belmont.

So instead, we tied a string to an arrow and shot it over the lighting grid waayyy up there."

"*Tuvimos que hacerlo desde el punto más alto. Peke.*" Dante pointed at the tower of trash behind them.

"Yeah. And then we got the arrow back with the string, and tied that to a long ball of twine."

"*Y tiró de la cuerda original hacia arriba sobre la rejilla,*" Dante gestured up again.

"And then we tied that twine to a wire, and then to a knotted rope…" Martin continued.

"*Y otra vez. Cambio. Repetir.*" Dante finished.

All eyes stared disbelieving at the twins.

"Okay. So how did that help?" Harry asked.

"Oh yeah, so once the rope was in place, Dante climbed up to the grid with a long line of spliced together charge cords hooked on his belt. Then connected it to a live wire up there, dropped the cord and…"

"*¡Ahí estamos! ¡Tienes poder!*" Dante finished.

They all looked dumbfounded first at the twins, then at the cord, and then their necks all craned upwards to follow the line. All. The. Way. Up.

"So you two were busy then." Gilly said.

Both twins grinned proudly under their gaze.

"Yes. Well busy or not – does it work?" Rachel said.

Dante held up the cord as Belmont offered the phone.

"Oh no, they don't fit!" Belmont said dejectedly.

"*Ahora espera un minuto. Tenemos un plan de copia de seguridad,*" Dante said, scrambling through his pockets. He pulled out a jumble of wires, connectors and adapters and fiddled with the end of the phone. One clicked in, and he connected the long cord that connected to heaven.

They waited again, and for a few seconds nothing happened.

Still nothing.

And still nothing.

"What if…" Harry started.

Suddenly, a faint orange light blipped once, then twice and then it burned soft but beautifully.

Martin and Magnus hugged. Gilly squeaked and Rachel leaned in to give Belmont a kiss.

A real live kiss.

Belmont thought their cheer could be heard on Morge Mountain. But he didn't care. He screamed right along with them as the group hugged and jumped around in a circle.

Let them hear, he thought happily. We're going home soon!

Next?

"Is it charged up yet?" Apple asked for the tenth time.

"Not yet. We have to give it a couple more minutes." Belmont responded, again. "They don't take a charge right away. It takes some time."

"But it will work right? I mean, in just a few more minutes?" Gilly pleaded.

"It's prolly okay if it don't work." Apple said.

Belmont stared at the orange flashing light a bit longer without responding. Then he said, "All right. It's time."

The phone felt heavy in his hand. He stroked it tenderly with his thumb before pressing the on-button.

The screen of the obsolete phone flickered and then came on.

"It works?! It works! Does it really work?" Rachel was uncommonly excited.

Belmont looked up happily and nodded.

"Oh MY G... Do we call? Who do we call? The police? The fire department. Do you know the number for the World Health Organization?" Harry was stammering.

"Yes. The phone works, yes. But, hold on. Look here. Oh. Oh no.... Oh, of course. Of course that's a problem." Belmont was talking to himself.

They all stared at him with confusion. Someone broke the silence: "So what? What's up? What's wrong??"

"Of course this is a problem down here. We're miles underwater. I should have known – Louis even told me so. Of course, it doesn't work. We can't get service. We can't get a signal way down here."

They all stared slack-jawed at him. "What does this mean? I thought it worked? Talk to us," Rachel said through clenched teeth.

"*¿La batería necesita más carga?*" Dante tried.

"We're not going to get a signal down here," he looked around at everyone.

"Are you kidding me?! The phone won't work? We wasted all of that time and…"

Rachel cut him off "…and risked our lives – and the phone won't even work??"

"No, wait. I didn't say it wouldn't *work*. But it won't work *down here*." Belmont looked around at everyone and then his eyes followed the cord up to the grid hanging above and then drifted to the Canyon Rim far in the distance.

"It will work, but we need to go up. Up up. To the UpTop," he looked at Harry and then to Rachel.

"I hope you didn't use up your appetite for adventure because we need to figure out a way to get to the top. Then the phone will work. That's where we can call. That's where we will get saved."

THE END